To
the villagers of Hallsands village
in South Devon,
who lost their homes and livelihoods
on the night of 27th January 1917.

And in memory of
Claude and Lawrence Garnett,
died in Mesopotamia and France
December 1915 and November 1917,
two among seven million young men
– husbands and sons and lovers –
who lost their lives in the Great War.

1

I'm old now. I live alone in my bungalow, looking out over the sea that has been my friend and enemy these last ninety-five years. It's very comfortable here, and I have my dog Judy for company. On sunny days we walk down to the beach, and watch the children build sandcastles, the gulls, the sparkle on the waves.

It isn't always like that. Last winter there was a terrible storm, and the sea came across the road and smashed the windows on the old houses near the harbour. A tanker was wrecked at Gammon Head, and the crew had to be winched off with helicopters. I watched it on the evening news.

Not everyone's so lucky, even now. The sea gives and the sea takes, and many good men lie at the bottom of her, never found and never buried. My brothers, Trevor and Jacob, for example, who went out fishing one morning in 1937, and never returned. I still look out to sea sometimes and see a little vessel, and wonder if it's them, coming home after all. It couldn't be, of course; they'd be nearly a hundred. And just last week I read in the paper about a father and son who were caught in a storm in their sailing dinghy. The rescue service found the boat, but they never found them. They were only having a holiday.

It happened then and it happens now.

*

I grew up in a fishing village called Hallsands, on the other side of the headland, the side that's sheltered from the west wind. There were two rows of cottages, with a post office, a shop and an inn, perched on a rock ledge. There wasn't a proper road to it, just a track along the top of the beach, and a zigzag path up the steep cliffs. In fine weather we came and went by boat, across the bay. We hauled the boats onto the beach: our beach, where the fishermen sorted their catches and made lobster pots and mended nets, where the women hung out the washing, where dogs and chickens nosed after scraps, where we played.

I was the youngest of the family. My mother kept the post office, and my father was away in the navy, fighting in the Great War. My older brothers went out with the fishing boats. A lot of the young men were away at the war, so the older ones and the boys did the hard jobs. And the women. There was nothing the women didn't do in those days in a fishing village.

They were kind people at Hallsands, knowing all about each other's business and tolerating most of it. There must have been lots of children, but I don't really remember them. I remember John, though. John Mingo. He was my best friend, a year or so older than me – tall and strong and terribly handsome, I thought. He's still alive too, living in the nursing home at Kingsbridge.

I ought to go and see him one day, see if he remembers.

2

'Sarah! Take your nose out of that book and do something useful for a change.'

'Like what, Mam?'

'Like making the bread for me, or cleaning out the fire...'

But it was a brisk spring day. If I couldn't be reading, I'd rather be outside. And I could see John Mingo helping pull his father's boat up the beach.

'Can I go out with John, Mam?'

'All right. But mind you bring something back for our supper!'

That shouldn't be too difficult. There was plenty to eat along the shoreline. There were crabs and mussels and prawns. We'd take John's dog, Skip, and with a bit of luck she might get a rabbit. If nothing else, we could always take a pair of scissors and snip the new shoots of nettles, for a soup.

But John had other ideas.

'The seagulls are nesting up the point, Sarah. Let's have a go at getting some eggs! I'll do the climbing,' he added, looking down at me and reminding me that I was after all only a girl, and a year younger than him too.

We headed up towards the point, then cut across the rocky tors to the west side. The wind hit us hard on the top there, so we could lie against it using our coats as sails, looking back at the calm water of the bay. We could see our village nestling under the cliffs, snug and out of the wind. Skip lay low and sheltered in the bracken.

There was a ship in the bay.

'What's that doing?' I shouted over the wind.

'Dredging for shingle,' John shouted back.

'What for?'

'They're building new docks in Plymouth. Massive great things. Reckon they need all the shingle they can get.'

'There's plenty of it anyway,' I said. 'Enough for everybody, I should think.'

'That's not what my dad says,' shouted John. 'My dad says it'll lower our beach and let the sea in, and we'll all be flooded.'

I looked down at the village, so safe and snug, with smoke coming from the chimneys and little figures busy on the beach. It didn't seem possible.

'They've built the new wall, though,' I said. 'That'll keep us safe.'

John pulled in his coat tails and dipped his head, turned quickly and ran down the grassy slope to the cliff top.

The gulls took off when they saw us.

They came up in a great cloud, squawking and wheeling: kittiwakes, herring gulls and fulmars. It was the fulmars that we were after. We lay on the cliff edge, looking over, while they dive-bombed us. We could see the nests and the eggs in them.

'You can't climb down there,' I said.

'No, stupid, we don't climb down. We climb up.'

He pointed to a ridge of rock. From the bottom, where the waves crashed on big boulders, you could work out a way to climb it that would take you right in among the nests.

'You've done it before?' I asked.

'Of course I have,' he said. 'My brother showed me.'

'Don't your mam mind? It looks dangerous.'

He shrugged and gave me a look and I wished I hadn't said it. The Mingos had been living on this coast since time began, practically, and the boys had always climbed after seagulls' eggs. I could bet his mother didn't know what he was up to, though.

'Come on,' he said. 'First thing we've got to do is get down there.'

We followed the top of the cliff till we came to a gully, where we could get down. We half slid the first bit, and then scrambled down to the tidemark. Skip stayed up at the top, nosing after a rabbit. Dogs have a bit more sense than humans, sometimes.

The tide was out. We both knew that of course. We always knew where the tide would be, without having to think about it.

We had to go below the tidemark, where the rocks were wet and slippery, so we stepped carefully. The sea

5

was crashing against the boulders just below us, and every so often an extra big wave would lift a plume of foam high in the air, and it would blow over and drench us. We didn't mind. It was fun.

We scrambled along till we were right underneath the fulmar nests. Skip had run along the top of the cliff, keeping one eye on us and one on her rabbit, and we could sometimes see her up there, way above us. The gulls wheeled in tight circles, squawking and diving at us. They knew what we were about all right.

There was a small beach in between the rocks, with round pebbles that were brightly coloured in the wet of the sea-spray. I gathered a handful and looked at them, thinking I could take some back for my little garden. I picked out one in particular – a beautiful shiny green stone, ground to a perfect oval by the sea – and slipped it into my pocket.

But John's mind was on eggs.

'That's the way!' he said, pulling my arm and pointing upwards.

It was quieter here, because the rocks sheltered us from the wind, though there was still the roar of the sea behind us.

I looked up. For the first time, I was pleased he'd said I wasn't climbing.

'It's too steep, John,' I said. 'What if you fell?'

He gave me another of his looks.

'Mingos don't fall,' he said.

'What do they do, then, fly?' I snapped back.

But John wasn't listening. He was trying the rock for hand grips.

And a moment later he was off, not looking down, his coat tails flapping, gripping the rock like it was his mother, and moving hold by hold up the spur, testing each bit of rock before he put his weight on it.

Watching him, I thought: He's right. Mingos don't fall.

Far up above, Skip was jumping backwards and forwards and barking in excitement, while the gulls yelled in fury.

John was at the nests now. The gulls were shrieking and diving at him, but he took no notice, just stretched for the nearest nest, took an egg and slid it carefully into his pocket.

He took off his cap and waved down to me, grinning happily.

He reached for another. This one was above him. The mother gull was flapping in his face as he twisted and pulled himself up.

He was at the top of the hard granite, reaching the shale above it. He was so excited with getting the eggs, that he forgot to test the rock, and didn't realise it was loose.

He stretched out to wave at me again.

'Watch out!' I yelled.

He didn't hear. He couldn't have heard anything over the screaming of the seagulls and the roar of the sea.

The next thing that happened, the rock came away

and he was tumbling down towards me, knocking against the cliff as he fell. He might have screamed. I couldn't hear, because I was screaming myself. But his coat tails were flying up behind him, like wings.

3

'John!' I screamed. 'John!'

I ran up to him. I was sure he was dead.

I knelt beside him.

'John! Wake up!'

There was a cut across his forehead, and his face was white. But he was still breathing.

I shook his shoulder, which was a stupid thing to do. It might have hurt him more. But I didn't know any better.

'John!' I sobbed. I took his cap, which had fallen beside him, and filled it with seawater from a pool, and threw it over his face.

It worked. He stirred.

He opened his eyes and looked around, trying to make sense of things.

'What happened?' he muttered.

'You fell, John. You fell off the blooming cliff.'

He lifted an arm, watching it to make sure it was doing what it was supposed to do. He reached into his coat pocket, and pulled out a sticky mess of yolk and eggshell.

'I bust the egg, Sarah,' he said, trying to smile. 'I'd better go up and get another one.'

Then he tried to stand up.

He got as far as his knees, then he fell backwards, groaning.

'Are you all right, John?' I asked stupidly.

I was looking at his leg. There was something wrong about it.

He wasn't listening to me. He was being sick. I can remember exactly what it looked like: a froth of green and orange bits, spreading out across those pretty stones.

When he'd finished, a little colour came back in his face, and he asked me to help him sit up against the rock. I had to drag him a bit. It must have hurt him terribly, but he never made a sound.

I took off my coat and put it behind him to lean against. At least we were out of the wind.

'What are we going to do, John? You'll never get back across the rocks.'

'I'll be all right in a minute,' he said.

'You won't,' I said. 'You've broken your leg. You'll never walk like that. I'd best go and get help.'

'You won't have time. The tide's coming in.'

It was. There was a boulder back towards the gully, and I stood on it and looked at the swell. It wouldn't be long before the waves were crashing against that boulder, and foaming round the pebbly beach where John lay.

'I'll run,' I said.

He looked at me with panic in his eyes.

'Don't leave me now, Sarah. Get me higher first.'

He started to struggle to his feet again, but fell back, pulling a face at the pain.

'Just a minute. I'll do it in a minute,' he grunted through his teeth.

I was desperately trying to think of a way to get help. Or hoping someone would come. But no one even knew we were there.

Then I thought of the dog.

I could see her above us on the clifftop. Perhaps she could get help for us.

'Skip!' I shouted. 'Go and get someone. John's hurt. Quick!'

She heard me, at least, and started jumping up and down and barking, but that was all. She wasn't a specially obedient dog anyway, and I couldn't expect her to understand me.

I sat down next to John. I thought, We'll just have to sit here together and drown. That made me want to cry, but crying wouldn't have helped anything, so I fought it back. Then I remembered I had a humbug in my pocket that my mother had given me for helping in the post office, so I gave it to John. He put it in his mouth, and lay back against the rock and shut his eyes. He looked as if he was going to sleep.

I shut my eyes too. Perhaps if I kept them shut long enough it would turn out to all be a dream.

A wave hit the rock in front of us, and the spray drenched us.

John opened his eyes.

'We've got to move,' he said. 'Come on! We'll do it this time.'

'Just get to the top of that boulder,' I said. 'It'll give us more time.'

11

John nodded.

I helped him up, and eventually he got balanced on his good leg, leaning heavily on me. But every step we hopped, I could feel him holding back the scream.

We managed a few steps across the pebbles, but then the wind hit us. We looked out at the way we'd come earlier, scrambling so easily over the wet rocks.

'Come on, John!' I said. 'It's not far.'

The tide had come in, and fingers of foam were reaching up round the rocks.

'I can't do it,' said John, gritting his teeth against the pain. 'You go!'

'I can't go without you!' I said.

I felt him sliding down against me and let him fall back onto the pebbles.

'Go on!' he said. 'You can get help.'

I looked at him. His face was white and tense, and his leg was twisted. He was soaked through, we both were.

The roar of the sea was louder here, and the seagulls were screeching again. I wanted to scream with them.

'I'm not leaving you here,' I shouted, clenching my fists. 'Get Up! Get Up!'

A wave smashed against a rock just below us, and the foam rose up in a plume and crashed down on us like a shower. It didn't matter. We couldn't get any wetter.

'I can't,' he said. 'I can't go any further.'

I was terrified, for myself as well as him. But I couldn't leave him there. I just couldn't.

'You can crawl, can't you?' I yelled at him. 'Just

crawl to that boulder, and I'll pull you up it!'

'I can't, Sarah,' he sobbed. 'It hurts too much!'

There was a sudden lull, and I thought I heard Skip barking. I looked up behind me, and then my heart leapt.

Skip was still there, jumping about and barking; and next to her, silhouetted against the sky, was a man. One hand was raised to his forehead against the dazzle from the sea, and he was looking down at us.

4

I leapt up and down, shouting and waving. The man waved back, but the din of the wind and the waves had started again, and he probably couldn't hear me.

Then he turned and vanished from my view.

I panicked. He was going away and leaving us. Or he was going to get help that would be too late in coming.

I looked at John, helpless on the wet pebbles.

'I'm coming back,' I said.

Then I ran, jumping from rock to rock, back to the gully. I slipped badly, cutting my leg, but although I saw the blood I didn't feel any pain. I just kept going till I got to the gully. Then without even looking up I scrambled up it, tugging too hard at tufts of grass that came away in my hand, so that I nearly lost my balance. Little rivers of gravel tumbled down behind me.

I was almost at the lip of the clifftop when I missed my footing. I fell against the slope, and grasped at whatever I could, but I felt myself sliding back down.

'Steady on!'

A hand grasped mine. A big strong hand, that pulled me back up till I was sitting gasping at the cliff edge, with Skip jumping up at me and licking me.

'Get your breath back, then tell me what's happened.'

It was the man. He'd come along the cliff looking for a way down. I looked up at him, and my fear ebbed away. He was here! He would save us!

He didn't meet my eyes. He looked past me as if he was watching for something. And then I felt shy, because he wasn't like anyone I'd ever seen before. He was young, not much older than my brothers, and strong like them. But his face was quite different, pink and soft and rounded, almost like a baby. He had a little wispy moustache that only made him look younger.

'Are you all right?' he asked, noticing the cut on my leg. 'That looks like a nasty scratch.'

His voice was strange too, soft and tight at the same time. It was the first time I'd heard an upper-class voice. But there was something else about him too, something that in my half-panicked state I wasn't quite putting together.

'I'm fine,' I panted. 'The cut's nothing. It's my friend that's hurt. He was getting gulls' eggs and he fell. I think he's broke his leg. And the tide's coming in and he can't get out.'

He drew in his breath sharply.

'Can we get more help?'

I shook my head. 'The village is too far. The tide's coming up fast.'

'Then we'll have to do the best we can. Let's hope we can manage. Show me the way!'

I slid back down the scree to the bottom of the gully, then turned to watch him follow me. I realised then what was odd. His feet were sure and nimble, and his right hand caught at the grasses to steady his balance, but his

15

left sleeve was tucked permanently into his raincoat pocket.

He only had one arm.

By the time we got back to John the spray was wetting the little beach regularly.

The man knelt down, looking at John's leg.

'I'll bet that's painful,' he said. 'Let's have a closer look.'

John clenched his teeth as the man pulled up his trouser leg.

It was horrible. His leg was twisted half way down and you could see an edge of bone poking against the skin.

'Can you find some driftwood?' the man asked me. 'Not too big. We'll make a splint.'

There were plenty of bits of wood washed up from old wrecks among the rocks, and I soon collected an armful. When I got back, the man was bent over John, talking to him, and John was smiling.

I put the wood down beside him. He looked at it, then turned back to John.

'Right,' he said. 'This is going to hurt, but there's nothing for it. You'll just have to be brave. Then we can get you home.'

He took off his mackintosh, and helped John to lie on it. Then he pulled off his shirt too, leaving only a vest, and showing the stump of his arm. It tailed off from his shoulder, patterned with livid red scars.

I shouldn't have stared at it, but I couldn't help myself.

He felt me looking, and blushed.

'War wound,' he mumbled. He handed me his shirt.

'Tear that into strips!'

I took it. It was lovely soft cloth, far too good to tear up. I just held it, feeling it with my fingers, and went on staring at him in his vest, with his stump of a left arm and pink cheeks, and the sea spray splashing around us.

'Hurry up,' he said impatiently, and started examining the driftwood. He chose some strong thin bits and put them beside John. Then he made John lie back and put his leg out as straight as it would go. John screamed, then stopped himself.

'Sorry,' he said.

'Don't be sorry,' said the man. 'Here, take a bit of cloth. Bite on it if you need to.'

I'd finally torn the shirt into strips and gave one to John. The man took the rest and put them neatly next to the driftwood. He looked at me.

'Now do what I tell you! Hold onto him round the knee here. That's right, get your arms right round it, and hold on tight, whatever happens. All right, John, this won't take a minute. Ready, boy...?'

John grunted.

The man gripped his broken leg by the ankle. His hand was large and strong, and his arm was muscled up like my brothers' arms, but softer and paler. Suddenly he pulled and twisted at the same time.

John's scream was muffled by a mouthful of cotton. His leg was straight again.

Quickly, the man picked up a piece of wood and put it against the straightened bone of his leg.

'Hold that there!' he ordered.

He put another on the other side and I held that too. Then, using his arm and his mouth, he threaded strips of his shirt around them, to make a splint. But although he could pull the strips around the leg, he couldn't make a knot. I saw his fingers tense and his face redden, this time in frustration.

I bent past him, and pulled the knot tight. Then we worked together, till the leg was stiff and secure.

John's mouth was clenched tightly round the cotton, and there were tears in his eyes. But slowly his face relaxed, and at last he pulled the cotton from his mouth and breathed deeply again.

A wave hit the rocks and drenched us, and the after-wash foamed round our knees and John's back, washing away the remaining driftwood. We were so wet already we hardly noticed; nor the cold either, though John's teeth were chattering.

'Come on,' said the man. 'Time to move. Think you can do it?'

John nodded. The man bent down and put his arm under his back.

'Hold tight now. I've got you.'

He struggled up with John over his shoulder. The splinted leg stuck out awkwardly in front of him.

I picked up his sodden mackintosh, that John had been lying on, and went ahead of them.

The tide was higher, and the water was flushing around the rocks. But it was easy for me; I just scrambled along till I was at the bottom of the gully. Then I looked back.

With no hand to steady himself, the man was going one step at a time, carefully, slowly, completely concentrated on keeping his balance, not bothering how the water pulled at his legs.

John clung to his shoulders, his arms linked through the man's stump.

A plume of foam fanned behind them, reflecting rainbows.

5

Yesterday my grand-daughter came to visit. My children and grandchildren are spread out all round the world, but she lives quite close, in Exeter, and she often comes to see me. She's called Sarah, like me.

It was a fine day, and she wanted to take us out.

'Why don't we go over to Hallsands, Nan? Have a look where you used to live.'

'I don't think so,' I said.

I don't want to see those ruins, and I had my own ideas.

'Let's go to Plymouth,' I said. 'We can take Judy for a walk on the Hoe.'

'Good idea,' said Sarah, 'and then we can have a cream tea in the Barbican.'

A cream tea in the Barbican! How times change. The Barbican is a tourist centre now, with a marina and expensive restaurants, but I remember it as a slum, full of rats and drunken sailors. Then before that again, it was a thriving fishing port. But it still has something of the same smell, of fish and alcohol.

Plymouth Hoe is a grassy park looking over the bay and out to sea, where Sir Francis Drake played bowls, waiting for the Spanish Armada. I didn't tell Sarah why I wanted to go there. But we ended up where I knew we would: the War Memorial.

You couldn't call it beautiful. It's big and pompous like the politicians who put it there. On the top is written in big brass letters:

In honour of the navy, and to the abiding memory of these ranks and ratings of this port who laid down their lives in the defence of the empire and have no other grave than the sea.
Their Name Liveth Forever.

There's thousands of names. Each one a young life, snuffed out. Each one a family grieving at home.

Judy made friends with a little terrier, and they ran around happily, while I searched out a well-known spot.

The dead were listed by year, and then by rank:

Commander James Philpott
Midshipman Philip Drewry
Able Seaman Richard Addy
Able Seaman John Barnes . . .

The list went on and on and on.
I got out my glasses to see it better.
Sarah came up close.
'What are you looking at, Nan?' she asked.
I pointed to a name:

Able Seaman Edward Coleman

'That's your great-grandfather. My father,' I said.
She looked for a long while. We both did. Although

*there was nothing to look at, only a name stamped in
brass.*

'*I never knew,*' *she said softly.*

It was a long time ago.

6

I was lonely, with John in the hospital.

It wasn't that I didn't have plenty to do. I went to school. I helped my mam. I went fishing with the Trout girls. There were four of them and no brothers, but they were terrific at fishing; we came back with the boat laden with pilchard and mackerel and herring and crabs. But I missed John, and I couldn't stop wondering about the young man who'd rescued us – who he was, how he'd lost his arm, what he was doing out on the cliffs. I kept seeing his face in my dreams.

Mr Mingo tried to find out about him, but nobody knew him. He'd left us on the rocks above the tide line, run to the village wrapped in his soaking raincoat, and told them about us. Then he'd disappeared, like the rare birds that were sometimes blown in on a storm, were seen for a day, and went as suddenly as they came.

Every spare minute, I read. My schoolteacher lent me books and I read all of them. I didn't understand everything in them, but they were something special to me – a window to other worlds.

I read about battleships, like the one my father was on, and aeroplanes and submarines. I read about cities, and jungles, and mountain peaks, and the frozen wastes of the Antarctic. I read about wealthy people with

23

mansions and motor cars. I read about war.

When I came out of my book, the village seemed very small.

One morning I slipped off early before my mother could catch me and tell me to do something. I lingered by the London Inn. It was fine, and the men were sitting outside, talking – mostly the older men and a few big boys, the rest were away at the war. I don't know why Mr Mingo hadn't been called up; perhaps he was too old, or perhaps they needed to leave a few experienced fishermen.

'They've stopped the dredging, anyway,' said old Mr Fawkes. They had done too, mainly because Mr Mingo had been to see the Member of Parliament and shown him what was happening.

'Too late now,' said Mr Mingo. 'Look at our beach!'

The beach was still there, and the boats were dragged up on it, as they'd always been. In a storm they'd be pulled higher, behind the wall.

But it was smaller with every gale.

'It'll come back now they've stopped,' said Mr Fawkes. 'There's plenty of shingle in the sea where that came from.'

'And a dirty great hole further down the bay, that's going to fill up from our beach in the next storm. You'll see,' said Mr Mingo.

'They needed the shingle for the war effort, Dad,' said Tom, John's elder brother. He'd be joining the navy next year.

Mr Mingo glared at him.

'The war's to protect us from the Hun, not to drown us with our own stupidity. Go and make yourself useful, boy.'

I climbed up the steep cliffs behind the village, and went over onto the Point, near where we'd gone for the gulls' eggs. It was sunny, and when I squeezed down in the bracken I was out of the wind with just a blue sky and seagulls turning above me.

I lay and read a book, and in between reading I sat up and watched the sea for warships. We often saw them coming and going from the new docks in Plymouth, that were built from our shingle.

There was a convoy passing: warships in a line, and cargo ships between them. Perhaps my dad was on one of them, coming back to us. He'd been away for two years. I tried to remember what he looked like, but I could only remember what he felt like, his bigness and calmness in our little parlour. I liked thinking about him, though. It made me feel safe.

I yawned. I was about to lie back in the bracken, when I saw the man.

He moved, or I'd never have noticed him. He was lying among the rocks of a tor some way above the cliffs, looking through a pair of binoculars.

For a moment I thought perhaps he was spying for the Germans. Then I remembered his face, and I knew he wasn't. I wanted to get closer though, so I crawled along through the bracken, then climbed down to the tor.

There was a big rock straight above him. Being as quiet as I could, I crept out to its rim and looked down at him.

He was lying on his front, pressing his binoculars to his eyes. But he wasn't looking at the convoy.

Then suddenly he started, twisted around and jumped up, looking straight up at me. I stood up, feeling sheepish. He stared at me in alarm for a moment, then he relaxed and smiled.

'Oh it's you!' he shouted up. 'I thought for a moment . . . well, never mind. Are you alone?'

I nodded.

'Come on down!' he said.

I clambered down the rock to him. He'd found a sheltered place with a great view of the clifftops and the sea. He'd spread out his mackintosh to lie on, and a notebook was open in front of him with drawings of birds. He also had a bag with a thermos and a box of sandwiches.

'How's your friend – John, wasn't it?' he asked immediately.

'He's still in hospital,' I said. 'But he's getting better. They say his leg's going to be all right.'

He shook his head. 'He's lucky,' he said. 'Dangerous business, stealing gulls' eggs.'

'It's not stealing,' I said quickly. 'They don't belong to nobody.'

'They belong to the gulls,' he said, looking back out

to sea. 'Don't you love the gulls? Don't you love the way they bank and turn? Look out there!'

He pointed across the bay to where a flock of gannets were circling and dive-bombing into the water.

He held his binoculars to his eyes to see better.

'Did you ever see anything so beautiful as the way those gannets dive? That is flying!'

I saw them every day, and I didn't know what he was talking about. They just seemed ordinary. But then I looked again, and the way he showed them to me, they didn't seem ordinary any more.

'I used to fly like that,' he said. 'Just like that. You cruise high, and then you dive suddenly, firing like the blazes. Except then you pull out at the last minute, up and away as quick as you can, before some other blighter gets you. Well, I won't be doing that any more.'

'What do you mean?'

'I was a Birdman,' he said, still watching through his binoculars. 'You know. A flying ace. In France. Fighting the Hun.'

'The Hun' was what we called Germans. They were the Enemy.

He put down his binoculars and reached in his pocket.

'I'll show you something.'

He pulled out a medal: a cross stuck to some stripy material.

'See this?' he said. ' It's the Military Cross. They give it for bravery. They don't know anything.'

'You're a hero,' I said, awe-struck.

'A hero? No. No, it wasn't like that at all. Heroes are meant to be brave, aren't they? I wasn't brave. Stupid, more like. At least, I wasn't any different from any of the other fellows. Still, all that's over now. For me at least. Other chaps are still out there, of course, doing their bit for Blighty...'

He tailed off, and slipped the medal back in his pocket. Then he looked at me. He looked straight at me, and met my eyes. His eyes were grey-green, like the sea.

'What's your name?' he asked.

'Sarah.'

'Sarah. You've got a lovely, trusting face, Sarah.'

I blushed scarlet and then so did he. Then we both laughed and he looked away.

'I'm called Julian,' he said quietly. 'I come here to watch the birds.'

'Julian the Birdman,' I said slowly.

He smiled.

'Julian the Birdman, if you like.'

Far out to sea the convoy was steaming out of sight.

7

We sat on his mackintosh feeling the sun hot on our faces, and he gave me one of his sandwiches. It was made with white bread, and it had real cheese in it. I'd hardly ever had cheese before. It tasted strange, but I liked it. I felt relaxed, sitting there in the sun and munching away.

'Tell me about the war,' I said suddenly. 'What's it like to fly over all those guns and things? I bet it's exciting.'

He shook his head.

'You're too young,' he said

'I'm not!' I said indignantly. 'I'll be thirteen next birthday. And I read all about everything, all over the world.'

I showed him the book I was reading, about Captain Scott's journey to the South Pole.

'Go on!' I said. 'Please tell me! Tell me what it's like!'

He looked out to sea again.

'I can sit here,' he said, 'and imagine I'm in the sky over France. The wind's the same, whistling through your wings, always cold up at 10,000 feet. Then there's the roar of the waves hitting the rocks; it just takes a bit of imagination to think it's the Archies – the anti-aircraft guns on the ground. And you watch out for the Hun, but you can't hear him over all the other din, so he takes you

29

by surprise, comes in from behind, like you did just now. Then you wheel away and spin and dip and turn, till you've thrown him off your tail. And if you're lucky you get up above him, and get a shot back at him. Like a game. A great game.

'Only after every game, you count your chums, and there's a couple more faces missing.'

'I'll bet you were a good flyer,' I said. 'One of the best.'

He shrugged his shoulders.

'Perhaps. I always wanted to fly. Never wanted to do anything else, ever. I was at school when the Wright brothers made their first flight, and I knew immediately that that was what I wanted to do with my life. Then the war started, and they wanted pilots. Lucky for me, I thought.

'I signed up as soon as I left school. I won't ever forget the first time I went up. One moment you're bumping over the grass, and then the instructor pulls a lever and up she goes and you're over the trees looking down at the roads and the houses. Then later you take over the controls and... What a feeling! All my wishes coming true at once!'

He broke off and pointed at a hawk flying fast and low against the cliff face.

'A peregrine falcon! She's got a nest up on those crags somewhere, I'll bet.'

I looked, but I wasn't interested in the peregrine. I wanted to hear adventures.

'Tell me about fighting the Hun,' I insisted.

He looked at me with those grey-green eyes. I wasn't sure if he was really seeing me, though.

'There are some things it's better not to know,' he said quietly.

'I don't mind. Really I don't,' I said.

He turned towards the sea, staring out silently, as if he'd forgotten about me. The convoy had gone. A lone warship trailed its plume of black smoke, just this side of the horizon.

'Have you got anyone in the war?' he asked at last.

'My father's in the Royal Navy,' I said proudly. 'And my brothers are going next year.'

He paused, as if considering this, and then suddenly he started to talk. He didn't look at me. He was speaking to me but his mind was far away, as if he was out there in France, living it all over again.

'The training was jolly good, anyway. It wasn't just flying. We learned first aid, that's how I knew how to set your friend's leg. We learned French, because that's where we were going. One of the chaps suggested we should learn German, in case we were captured, but the rest of us weren't too keen on that idea. We didn't want to think about things like that. We just wanted to get to the war, and shoot Huns.

'I couldn't believe it when we first got to France. I thought it would be all rats and mud, but it was luxury. We were billeted in a castle, a few miles from the front. Waited on hand and foot, nothing to do all day except eat and sleep and sit under the trees chatting. And fly of course. Two patrols on most days. Out over enemy territory, dodging the Archies and the Whizzbangs, spying out troop movements, and shooting at the Hun when we saw him.

'As for the other chaps, I loved them. I loved them all. Only there was this thing, you know, when somebody didn't come back, and then the next day there'd be another fresh-faced fellow out from Blighty, to show the ropes to. Somehow I never got touched, myself, though I had some near scrapes. They called me Lucky. That was my nickname: Lucky!'

He laughed. But not because it was funny.

'And I shot down any number of Huns. I saw their faces sometimes before they dived. Boys like me. About to die. It didn't register – they were the enemy, after all. It was a game, and I was invincible.

'After three months there weren't too many left who'd come with me. Only my best friend, Harry.'

He took the medal back out of his pocket and stared at it for a while.

'I got this for Harry, you see. I keep it for him really.'

'I bet you saved his life, didn't you?' I asked eagerly.

He looked at me and narrowed his eyes.

'I killed a lot of people but I only ever saved one life, and that was your friend, not mine.'

Suddenly his face twisted up with pain. He pulled his jaw tight, so that the muscles stood out on his neck. His eyes were cold and hard.

'I'll tell you this, but you must never repeat it. Never.

It's a secret between us. Can you keep a secret?'

'Yes,' I managed to whisper.

'Then listen! Because I made a promise, and somebody has to know. The world isn't all larks and happy endings.'

He twisted away, shut his eyes and bunched his fist. And then he was back again in the skies over France, with the Archies and the Whizzbangs – and the Hun.

'We were flying in formation, six of us. Harry and I were the old hands, the other four had been out just a few weeks, very young and keen. We spotted a German two-seater over no-man's-land, heading back from taking photographs of our lines. The new boys whooped and raced down to put it out of its misery, but I knew the Hun's tricks by then, and peeled away upwards, to see if there were any Hun fighters waiting in the sun, to come down on us. Harry was flying next to me. He caught my eye and knew what I was up to, and he followed me.

'A moment later, and it was like a hornet's nest: ten at least of them, racing down at us, with the sun behind them blinding us.

'I yelled out, "Get above them!" Not that Harry could have heard in all that din, though he was only a few feet away from me. He knew what to do, though. We shot off in different directions, jigging and looping as the bullets whistled round us, gaining height to circle and come back at them.

'The other boys were popping away at the two-seater, miles below. They hadn't seen any of it. And most of the

33

Huns were diving down at them. Just a couple stayed on our tails.

'It was nothing to me. I did this every day. I banked and looped, hanging upside down for a moment and seeing the little puffs of smoke from the trenches far below me. Then I dived down at the Hun, firing like the blazes. I was coming in at an angle. I could see his face under his flying helmet. He looked round, to see where I was coming from.

'He only looked once. I gave a burst of my machine gun just before I banked, and saw him crumple. A moment later he was spinning down, with black smoke coming from his petrol tank. I dropped after him, then pulled out a few thousand feet lower as he crashed among the Archies. I raised my fist to salute the kill, and by a miracle, there was Harry alongside me, grinning and giving the thumbs up.

'The other boys were still below us. They had sunk the two-seater and peeled off, but the Hun had the advantage of height and numbers, and was charging into them. I saw one of our planes go down. Then I dived, with Harry just behind me, surprising them and making them turn.

'It was an awful dogfight: man to man and plane to plane, circling, manoeuvring, shooting, watching each other's tails. There were Huns everywhere, but we were the better flyers. I watched Harry shoot down two, and I may have bagged a couple myself.

'Then suddenly they'd gone, and the air was clear. We

34

were all counting, to see how many of us were left. There was Harry, and Rogers, and Hugnell, and myself... That was three missing. No, only two, because Smithson's plane was limping along in the distance, giving off white smoke, but sure to make it.

'I didn't really think about the missing, just then, or about their mothers or sisters. I certainly didn't think of the German mothers of the boys we'd killed. I just felt a great surge of triumph.

'We'd routed them!

'Harry went wheeling round on a Victory roll. I could see him above me for a moment, upside down, drunk on the joy of it.

'And as he came out of it, a lone mad Hun came dropping out of the sky, guns blazing...

'Harry's petrol tank went. I was right there, watching it. There was a sound like a crack, then a plume of flame heading downwards, and that was it: a hole where Harry had been, and a smoking patch on the ground. I thought I heard a scream. I might have heard a scream, but you can't be sure above the sound of the wind and the guns and your own engine. Probably it was just a scream in my own head.

'Rogers and Hugnell went after the Hun, and they got him all right, but I just flew back to base. I didn't have the stomach for any more.

'We were all heroes that night. The Commanding Officer put in a report and Harry and I got the Military Cross. Harry's was posthumous, of course. That means after you're dead. I don't know why we got it. It wasn't any different from any other mission, really.

'The C.O. didn't usually show any emotion – none of us did, we couldn't afford to – but he knew what was going on in me. He put his arm round my shoulder that evening in the mess.

'"I'm giving you a day off tomorrow," he said. "No use in brooding, but take it easy for a day or two."

'Take it easy? What did he know!'

9

'I had to find Harry, you see. I had to see him one last time.'

Julian stopped. He looked round at me, but he didn't seem to see me. It was more as if he was coming up for air.

'Do you have a friend – a real friend?' he asked.

I nodded. I was thinking of John.

'Then you'll understand me. Just the night before, a bunch of us had been in Boulogne. We'd been drinking a bit, flirting with the girls. Those French girls loved us Birdmen. It was never anything serious, of course. Just high spirits to take our minds off the danger. Anyway, after a while Harry and I left the rest of them and went out and sat by the docks, smoking, and looking at the stars reflected on the water. My dog was with us, and he put his head between my legs and I stroked his ears. I remember that. He was a scrawny, yellow thing, who turned up one day at the mess, and latched onto me, but I was fond of him. I wonder what he's doing now. Latched onto some other blighter, I expect.

'"What'll you do when the war ends?" Harry asked suddenly, turning his big dark eyes on me. He was older than me.

'"Flying," I said. "I'll go on flying, one way or another. I couldn't live without flying. What about you?"

'He hesitated for a moment.

'"Oh, I don't know," he said. "A little farm in Devon. Something like that. Settle down there with a country girl and have lots of babies. That's where my people are, Devon. I wish you'd meet them. My parents, and my sister Rachel. It's a lovely place, and you'd like them. You and Rachel, I'm sure you'd hit it off."

'He reached round his neck, and brought out a locket that hung there on a chain. He opened it. There were tinted photographs of his parents and his sister.

'"I keep them with me. They don't get lost that way." He grinned, then he turned serious.

'"If we, you know, if I... If anything happens to me, will you go and see them? Talk about me, and how it was, the larks and, you know, the other bits too. You can spare my mother, tell her some sweet lie, but Rachel — I'd like her to know. Everything. The truth. I want someone to know. I want someone to remember... You'll do it, won't you?"

'"Of course," I said.'

Julian stopped, and lit a cigarette. He wasn't very good at it. He had a smart silver cigarette case that he fumbled to open with one hand. Then he had to put the matchbox between his knees before he could strike a light. I could see him getting tense about it, but I didn't try to help him. He wouldn't have liked it.

He turned to me, as if he'd suddenly remembered my existence.

'I shouldn't be telling you all this. I don't even know you, really.'

He drew on the cigarette.

'Perhaps that's why I can tell you,' he went on, ' – because I don't know you. I can't tell my friends, you see. I never told anybody yet.'

He gazed broodily out to sea. He sucked at his cigarette again and coughed.

'I don't even like these things anyway,' he said, and threw it away.

'Did you find him?' I asked intently. 'Did you find Harry?'

I had to know. And then again I didn't want to. I was afraid of what I might hear. But by then I couldn't have stopped him telling me anyway.

He paused for a long time, remembering.

'I knew where Harry's bus had gone down,' he said at last. 'Behind a shattered wood, in no-man's-land. I'd marked all the details of the landscape from the air hundreds of times, and I knew I could find the place. I wanted to go and fetch his body immediately, but the C.O. said it was too dangerous, and we should leave it to the infantry. They'd bring him back on the next push.

'But I had to see him. I just had to.

'After dinner I slipped away without anyone seeing me, and cycled through the dusk on a rickety French bicycle till I came to the lines. The guns were quiet that evening. Nobody stopped me or asked me who I was. I left the cycle when the ground got rough, and walked along the top of a parapet, looking down into a trench. There were soldiers in it, but they took no notice of me. There was distant rumbling but it was very quiet where I was. No war going on at all.

'I could see where the shattered wood was, ahead of me. I knew the exact spot.

'A voice called up: "If you don't want to get killed, why don't you come down here, sir?"

'A soldier was looking up at me. He was a little fellow, caked in mud, with a running sore on his lower lip.

'I climbed down into the trench. I thought I might as well. It led the way I was going.

'"It's quiet tonight, sir," said the soldier. "But you never know when it's going to start again. You're not from our regiment. What brings you to these parts?"

'"I'm an airman," I said. "My friend was shot down, just by the wood over there. I want a look at him."

'"I wouldn't if I were you, sir. That's no-man's-land, that is. Not a pretty place."

'Where we were standing wasn't pretty either. It had been fine weather lately, but there was still stinking mud six inches deep at the bottom of the trench. A couple of rats ran out of a dug-out, squealing, and then stood looking at us, not even bothering to run away.

'"I know," I said.

'But I didn't.

'I gave him a cigarette, and we stood there smoking together quietly for a few moments. Then he led me down the trench until I was at the nearest point to

Harry's bus. He seemed to know exactly where it was.

'"Don't hang around, sir. It's just over the barbed wire. If you're quick, you might get away with it."

'He stopped for a moment and held me with his eyes.

'"I saw it come down, sir. We watch you, you know. And I wanted to say, I wouldn't swap my place for yours any day. I haven't got the bravery, sir."

'He shuffled away and I climbed out into no-man's-land in the heavy dusk.

'The wind was blowing over from the German lines, and it brought a stench of death.

'I stumbled forward towards a line of barbed wire. I could see a way through where it had been cut. But something else made me look at it, much as I didn't want to: a body, strung across the barbed wire like a rag doll hung up to dry, head thrown back, eyes plucked out by the crows, stomach ripped open, a ghastly grin on the swollen face.

'For a moment I thought it might be Harry. But it was a German. A Hun. The Enemy. I could tell by the helmet.

'And an awful thought came to me as I stood there in the fading light: that was somebody too, once. With a mother. Or a wife. Knitting socks and sending off parcels, perhaps even at that very moment, somewhere in Germany…

'It might seem strange, but until that moment I'd never thought of the Germans as being real people at all. That's how I could kill them.'

*

41

Julian paused and stared out over the cliff, where a flock of pigeons were twisting a rapid path towards us.

He stared at the birds, and I stared at him. I couldn't take my eyes off his face that was so fresh and so painful at the same time. He knew so much of the world already. And I'd seen nothing but Hallsands.

But I saw that dead body in my imagination, and I felt sick.

'I found Harry's bus, what was left of it, and what was left of Harry too. His clothes had burnt off him and his face was unrecognisable, blown to pieces by shrapnel, but whether before or after he crashed, I couldn't say. The body was twisted and charred, no scrap of clothes left on him. The hands and feet had burnt away to stumps. The whiff of death lay all around. As the soldier said, it wasn't pretty.

'I stood staring, thinking, "This can't be Harry. I've come to the wrong place."

'Then I saw his locket.

'The light was just fading. Everything became unreal. I felt I had no past and no future, no friends, no family, just me and a charred corpse, and bits of broken aeroplane in the mud. I reached out and pulled the locket off his blackened chest, over the shattered remains of his head. By some miracle it hadn't been damaged at all. I've still got it.'

Julian pulled a golden locket from his pocket, and flipped it open. I looked over his shoulder at tiny, perfect pictures of a grey-haired couple and a lovely young girl.

'I should have returned it, but I couldn't quite bring myself to ...'

He stopped again. Something had caught his eye: the peregrine falcon, high up towards the sun.

'What happened?' I asked, still desperately wanting a happy ending. 'Did you get back all right?'

He laughed bitterly, and flicked the locket shut.

'Depends what you mean by all right. A shell went off. Piece of shrapnel took my arm away. I passed out, woke up in hospital on my way to Blighty. They told me the soldier who showed me the way came and got me. Saved my life and risked his own. For what it's worth.'

Suddenly the peregrine was diving down out of a clear blue sky, scattering the pigeons, grabbing mercilessly at one of them.

Julian stood up and shouted.

Startled, the peregrine let go its hold and circled away. A wounded pigeon fluttered down onto the clifftop, not far away.

Julian ran over and picked it up. He held the terrified bird in his big hand, his thumb over one wing. The other wing hung limp and useless.

I knew what he was going to do.

'Don't kill it,' I pleaded. 'I'll look after it. I'm really good with birds and animals and things. I'll take it home, and make it better.'

'You hold it,' he said, and I took it and clutched it to my chest.

His fingers stroked the back of its neck until it went very quiet in my hands. Then suddenly he pulled at its neck and twisted. I felt it jerk, and then the life go out of it.

'No!'

I meant to yell, but I choked, gazing up at him with tears in my eyes, though whether for the pigeon or for Harry or for him, I couldn't say.

'It's better that way,' he said gently, taking the little corpse back from me. 'A wounded bird has no chance.'

Together we scratched out a hollow under the heather and we laid it to rest, covering it with shale and peat.

Then I made a little cross out of sticks, and found a slate, and Julian scratched on it:

A. PIGEON
DIED OF WOUNDS RECEIVED IN BATTLE,
22nd JUNE 1916
R.I.P.

We stood for a moment beside the little grave. The flock of pigeons had re-formed, and circled round us again, as though in a last salute.

'Time to go,' said Julian.

Suddenly he seemed happy, and much younger, like a boy again.

I followed him back to his place among the rocks, and watched him fold up his mackintosh.

'Give my best wishes to John,' he said. 'He's plucky. I'm sure he'll make a good recovery. You know, that was something special for me, to save someone's life after taking so many.'

He picked up his notebook. Then he looked round at me.

'Shall we do a bit of flying?' he asked.

I didn't know what he was talking about.

'Come here!' he said, sitting back down. 'I'll show you something. You need wings to fly.'

I sat beside him. He tore a page from his notebook and started to fold it carefully, with delicate movements of his fingers pressing against the side of his leg. He worked patiently, fully concentrated, while I watched.

'I practised this in the hospital,' he said. 'Day after day. I had to prove to myself I could at least do something with one hand. Besides, there was nothing else to do. But I never had such a good place to fly one.'

He stood up, holding a paper aeroplane – perfectly folded, with wings and tail fins – even a cockpit.

Then we climbed to the top of the tors, where the wind caught us.

'Watch!' he said. 'If it reaches the cliff edge it'll catch the thermal and fly right out to sea.'

He held it up. He didn't throw it. He just let the wind take it.

It rose up immediately, and I thought it was going to soar away for ever. Then a gust knocked it sideways, and it spun and dived, landing just short of the cliffs.

Julian shrugged.

'Ah well! Can't win 'em all.'

He was standing very close to me. I could feel the warmth of his body.

'I'd better get back now,' he said gently.

He collected his bag and his mackintosh. Then he stood awkwardly for a moment, looking slightly past me.

'Perhaps we'll meet again. One day,' he said.

I stared up at him.

'Thank you for listening, Sarah. I hope you'll be happy in your life.'

Then his eyes met mine. He blushed and then he smiled.

But I couldn't smile back. I had too many thoughts.

He turned and sprang away across the crags, moving lightly, as if a weight had fallen off him.

I watched him till he was out of sight. Then I clambered down the cliffs and found his paper aeroplane.

It was still perfect.

9

'Do you remember him?' my grand-daughter Sarah asked, as we stood looking at my father's name on the war memorial.

But I don't really, though I have a photograph of him standing in his navy uniform. It's next to my husband's, on my bureau. I just remember his presence, the feel of him.

It must have been terrible when the news came of his death, but I don't remember it at all. Just the time after, when my mother was crying and crying, and all I wanted to do was escape.

I shook my head.

'Weren't there any letters or anything?'

'Letters? Oh yes. My mother had a whole pile of them. She burnt them all though, before she died.'

'Why did she do that, Nan?' Sarah sounded quite shocked.

I looked up at her. She looks lovely at the moment, Sarah does. She's just married and expecting her first baby, and she seems to glow from inside her.

'They were love letters,' I said. 'She had a right to take them with her.'

Sarah blushed. It's hard enough to think of your own parents being in love. Your great-grandparents seem a long, long way away.

'She did leave one letter,' I said. 'I'll show it you when we get home.'

We didn't have the cream tea in the end, because we'd spent so long at the war memorial. Sarah wanted to read all the names, as a mark of a respect to their memory, though you never could, there are so many. We had a cup of tea in my bungalow instead, and we looked at my father's photograph and I showed her the letter.

Dear Madam,

I am very sorry to have to inform you that Able Seaman Coleman 16788 RNR went missing, presumed dead, during enemy action on 1st July, 1916. While he was attending his duties on deck, a shell exploded near him, rendering him unconscious, and before help could reach him, the heavy seas washed him overboard. I'm afraid there is no hope for his survival. He was a fine sailor, and I held him in the highest regard. We shall all miss him very much. I tender my deepest sympathy in your very sad bereavement.

Yours faithfully,
Comdr F. Stainton, Captain, HMS Hampshire.

Sarah read it several times, blinking away the moisture from her eyes.

'How old was he?'

'He was thirty-seven years old. My brothers were fourteen and fifteen. I was twelve.'

'It seems so sad,' she said.

'It was sad,' I said.

And then I thought: I've lived too long. I've seen too many loved ones die.

I must go and see John Mingo, in his nursing home, before he goes – or I do.

10

'Mam! Hey, Mam! Come out and have a look! The beach has moved again.'

But my mother didn't come. She was cleaning the clock. After my father died she couldn't stop cleaning up, and she never went out any more. We must have had the neatest house in the South Hams.

There was a crowd out on the wall. The wind had shifted round to the east, and there'd been a storm in the night. The waves were still crashing in, though the wind had dropped. Mr Mingo's face looked stern.

The beach had dropped by a yard.

'There's still plenty left,' said Mr Fawkes. 'Look, the tide didn't even touch the wall.'

'You're a fool, Jim Fawkes,' said Mr Mingo, and turned and strode away.

I couldn't stop thinking about the Birdman, and that story he'd told me. I didn't tell it to anybody else – never. I couldn't. I'd promised. It stayed inside me, and I couldn't get it out of my head: Harry, and dogfights in the air, and the Hun. It got mixed up inside me with the talk of the war and my mother's crying, and I had nightmares of screaming aeroplanes and charred hands and black, broken faces.

Whenever I could, I went up to the crags. I was sure

he'd be there again one day, with his binoculars, watching the gannets.

But though the gannets came back, he didn't. I sat in the hollow where he'd talked, and thought about him, and the war, and Harry, and I kept thinking he'd appear over the rock above me, and give me that shy smile and talk to me again. Only he'd tell me nice things this time. I wondered about his lost arm, how he was managing, whether you'd ever get used to it.

Sometimes I thought about my father, but I had to stop myself. It was too hard.

After a while I knew he wasn't coming back. But I went and sat in the hollow anyway. It was comforting.

I had a little garden that I'd made myself, tucked between the house and the cliff, and one morning I went there and started arranging pebbles. I still had the green stone that I found when John broke his leg, and I'd collected some round black ones. I made a special pattern with them and some white and orange ones that came from our beach.

I looked up, and there was John. He'd been back from the hospital for a while, and he'd had his plaster off the day before. He was fine. He still had a bit of a limp, but he did everything.

'What's that for?' said John, looking down at me doubtfully.

'It's not for anything. It's my garden.'

'You can't have a garden here,' said John. 'There's no earth. Plants don't grow without earth.'

But there was earth. I'd brought it there, making little pockets in the cracks in the rock, enough to grow sea thrift and thyme and primroses and forget-me-nots, among my collection of pebbles and seashells. It wasn't much, but it was all mine. I thought it so pretty.

'Guess what?' said John. 'Skip's had her puppies. There's four of them. Do you want to see them?

They were in a box in his front room. Skip was lying flat out with her tongue lolling, while they sucked at her. She wagged her tail and looked up at us, as if to say 'Aren't I clever!', while the little puppies wriggled all over her.

'You can have one if you want, when they're bigger,' said John.

I looked with longing.

'My mam wouldn't let me,' I said.

Mrs Mingo was hovering behind us.

'Come along, give her a bit of peace and quiet now. Out you go.'

We walked along the sea wall, watching the waves roll up what was left of the beach.

'I wonder what happened to the man,' said John. 'You know, the one who rescued us. My dad says no one's seen him again.'

'I have,' I said. It was the first time I'd told anyone.

John looked at me, surprised.

'He was a Birdman,' I said. 'Out in France fighting the Hun. I met him on the cliffs and he told me.'

John looked impressed.

'I'd like to see him,' he said. 'Perhaps he'd like a puppy. What was he doing on the cliffs, then?'

'He watches the gulls. He don't shoot them or look for eggs, he just watches them through his binoculars. It's because he can't fly himself any more, that's what I think. And he's a bit shy. He don't want to talk to people.'

'Well I want to talk to him,' said John. 'Let's find him. Show us where you saw him.'

Perhaps he'd be there, I thought, now that I had John with me. But as usual there was no sign of Julian along the cliffs. We saw some seals though, enjoying themselves in a bay that was out of the wind, hauling up onto the rocks, grunting and splashing around in the midday sunshine.

We lay and watched them for a while.

'He's probably staying with relations while he gets over the shell shock,' said John.

'What's shell shock?'

'It's what they get when a bomb goes off near them. They walk around all funny for a bit, and can't tie their shoelaces, and jump when they hear a bang.'

'I bet it's a lot worse losing an arm,' I said.

'I'll say. He was brilliant though, the way he straightened my leg and put the splint on and all.'

'Did it hurt?'

'Not half. But they said in hospital, he'd done it good. I wish I could see him again.'

We lay there watching a pair of young seals playing tag around the rocks. But John's brow was furrowed. He was thinking.

'Listen,' he said at last. 'We can find him, someone like that. He's gentry, isn't he? He was an officer. He'll be staying in a big house somewhere. There aren't that many of them. Let's go to one and ask. Come on! It'll be a lark anyway.'

I laughed. Trust John to think of something like that! And then I felt shy. He wouldn't want to see us again, would he, two children from the fishing village? He'd say he didn't know us...

And then I didn't care.

I jumped up, startling the seals.

'Get yourself moving, John Mingo!' I said. 'What are we waiting for?'

11

We walked for miles. And then it was the wrong house. I knew that at once, because I couldn't imagine Julian there. It was tall and grey and grim, with overgrown formal gardens and rooks in the trees. We went up to the back, where the laurels wrapped around the outbuildings.

There were some steps up to the back door. We hesitated, because it looked so forbidding, but at that moment a woman came out and shouted at us, calling us 'thieving brats'. I would have run away, but not John. He walked up the steps looking dignified, while I hung behind.

'We're not thieving,' he said, taking his cap off. 'We're just looking for a gentleman.'

The woman softened a little.

'Well, there's no gentlemen here, my boy,' she said. 'Not since the young master died in France, and the old master died of grief. Only her ladyship's left, and she near eighty and not so right in the head. No, no. You won't find no gentlemen here.'

'He's a young gentleman with one arm,' John persisted. 'Do you know if there's any other houses he might be staying at?'

'Couldn't tell you, I'm sure. You could try Colonel Featherstone, I suppose, at Kelston Grange. They've got a young lady there. Perhaps she has visitors. Get away with you now.'

'Where is that?' asked John.

But she'd finished with us.

'Can't you see I'm busy? Get off with you!'

She shut the door firmly, then watched us through a dirty window, to make sure we went.

'Where is it then, Kelston Grange?' I asked when we were back in the road.

'Haven't a clue,' said John.

'Let's go home. We can look again tomorrow.'

But John was determined. It was like with the eggs. He'd set his mind to it and you couldn't stop him.

'See that hill,' he said. 'We'll climb to the top. You'd see a long way from up there.'

He was right. It was hard to get up, pushing through brambles and bracken on an overgrown cart track, but once there we could see the whole area, a rumpled patchwork quilt of woods and fields, from Dartmoor to the sea.

I didn't think of it as beautiful. It was the only place I'd ever known.

'There! Look! That could be it!'

In the wooded valley directly below us there was an old gabled house, surrounded by terraced gardens, with a stream and lawns and shrubs, and acres of woodland, and a long, winding drive.

'Worth a try anyway,' said John.

*

We walked up the drive. The trees were full of birds.

There was nobody about. I was nervous, but John wasn't, and he went up to the front door and knocked, bold as brass.

We stood there for a while. There were some shuffling noises inside, then the door opened.

I stepped back and put my hand to my mouth. A grey-haired couple stood there, and I knew exactly who they were.

'Hello,' said the woman, with a hint of surprise. 'What can we do for you?'

We must have looked a sight to them: two poor children they'd never seen before. Our clothes were clean enough, but they were old and patched – they'd done several brothers and sisters before us and you couldn't get the smell of fish out. What's more, we were flushed and scratched from the brambles on the hill.

John took his cap off.

'Excuse me, ma'am, but we were looking for a gentleman called Mr Julian, because he helped us and we wanted to say thank you. He's an airman and ...'

He broke off because his words had had an effect. The couple were looking at each other.

'Thank you for what exactly?' said the woman.

'Well,' said John. 'It's like I was birds'-nesting and I fell off the cliff and he was looking at the birds, and he saw, so he saved me. I might have been taken off by the sea if it wasn't for him.'

The man chuckled.

'Well, well, well!' he said. 'Why don't you come in and tell us some more.'

They led us not into the kitchen as I expected, but into their drawing room. I'd never been in a room like that before. It was a big room, full of strange objects from other parts of the world, and paintings on the walls. There was a grand piano, and French windows out onto the lawn.

'Sit down! Please sit down!'

We looked for a bench or something that we were used to, but there wasn't one, so we sat down awkwardly on the armchairs.

John caught my eye and winked.

'Beth!' called the woman. 'Bring the children some lemonade. And some scones. I'm sure they're famished.'

She was a big woman, and her husband was little. He didn't look like a Colonel. He had wispy grey hair and kind eyes.

I looked round the room. Then I saw the photograph.

A young man in a flying helmet, with a black moustache and his head on one side, holding his hands in the air and laughing. So gay, so dashing, so alive...

It was Harry of course. I knew it must be, because I'd recognised his parents from the locket that Julian showed me.

The maid brought in lemonade and scones and gave us a look as if to say, 'What are you two doing sitting here, while I have to wait on you?', though it wasn't our fault. Then Mrs Featherstone asked John about Julian, and how he had rescued him.

John mumbled. He never could tell a story. Besides he was busy with his scones and lemonade.

But I couldn't touch mine. I sat there, completely still, staring at that face that looked so alive and was so dead. I kept imagining it all shattered, the hands burned to blackened stumps, the smell...

Colonel Featherstone noticed me staring, in the end.

'That's our son, Harry,' he explained.

I was going to say 'I know', but stopped myself in time. I wasn't supposed to know.

'Julian is Harry's friend,' explained Mrs Featherstone. '*Was* Harry's friend,' she corrected herself.

'He died in France,' said the Colonel, shaking his head.

'He was a hero,' said Mrs Featherstone. 'He died in action. Julian told us, bless him. He was with him, and he saw it all. He even went with the party to recover the body and he said Harry had an expression on his face of perfect peace... Why, what's the matter?'

I couldn't help it. I was thinking of the charred hands, and I burst into tears. They just came rolling out of me like a river.

John spoke for me.

'You see, ma'am, it's her father. He was killed too, just a few weeks back...'

'Oh, my poor child.'

And a moment later I felt Mrs Featherstone's arms around me, hugging me to her generous bosom.

'We're all together in this,' she murmured, almost to

herself. 'We've all lost someone, haven't we?'

I didn't know what I was crying for any more. Everything seemed to be getting mixed up in my head. So I stopped, and pulled away from her.

'I'm all right now,' I sniffed. 'I'm sorry.'

Mrs Featherstone stood up and walked over to the photograph of Harry.

'He was a wonderful son,' she said. 'He was everything a mother could wish for. Handsome, kind, clever, and affectionate. And brave. So brave. My brave, glorious boy. We can't have him back, but we can be so proud of him. I'm sure that's how you feel too, about your father. They are both in heaven now. It is a sweet and noble thing, to die for your country.'

She stood with her back to us, gazing at the picture.

'Mr Julian's not here at the moment, I'm afraid,' said the Colonel. 'He's with his parents, near London. He'll be back next week, though. I think the air suits him here. He's getting much better. Why don't you come round to tea, next Tuesday, and you can see him then. We'd like to have you to tea, wouldn't we, Margaret?'

'Oh yes,' said Mrs Featherstone, turning back to us. 'Do come to tea! Come next Tuesday! Julian will be back then.'

As we stood up to leave, the door opened, and a girl walked in. I looked at her with my mouth half open. I thought she was the most beautiful girl I had ever seen.

'Oh hello, Rachel,' said the Colonel. 'These two children are friends of Julian's. He gets up to all sorts of things that we don't know about when he's off on his walks . . . '

'I know,' said Rachel. 'I was listening.'

She was really lovely. I'd seen her picture in the locket that Julian showed me, but she looked much better in the flesh. She was slim, with long brown arms and delicate fingers, and dark curly hair, tied loosely back. She had a simply cut dress, but it was expensive material, green and shiny, and it showed off her figure beautifully. It was her face that was so special though, full of life and changing every moment, like the sea on a windy day. She must have been about sixteen.

'Rachel is Harry's sister,' said Mrs Featherstone.

'Harry was my brother,' said Rachel quickly.

'The children are just going. Perhaps you could set them on their way to Hallsands?'

'That's what I came in for,' said Rachel.

There was a prickliness between them as if they wanted to shout at each other but were too polite.

They showed us to the door, and Rachel led us down the drive, walking fast. John, with his limp, was struggling a bit to keep up.

Rachel noticed, and stopped suddenly.

'Is your leg hurting?' she asked.

'Not really,' said John, never one to complain. Rachel looked him up and down, then walked on, more slowly.

'You live in that fishing village, don't you? Hallsands. You don't know how lucky you are.'

Neither of us knew what to say to that. We had a

decent life in the village. The work was hard, but there was enough to eat, most of the time, and we had nice homes. But our clothes were patched and re-patched, and we had none of the luxuries we'd seen in her house. We took it for granted that the gentry were the lucky ones, not us.

She saw that we didn't understand.

'You have friends,' she said. 'You have adventures. You go out fishing and climbing cliffs. I just hang around here doing nothing, while the boys go off to the war, have larks and get killed. Like Harry. You see these gardens? That's what my father does. He created them himself after we came back from India, when Harry and I were quite little. It's all he cares about now. And my mother plays the piano and stares at Harry's photograph. But what am I supposed to do? I'm young. I couldn't care less about gardens and pianos. I want to have a good time and see the world. But I'm stuck here, while Harry goes and dies a hero in France. It's all right for him, he's out of it. But I have to stay here for ever, till I'm wrinkled and ugly and sour.'

I had to say something. It was those blackened stumps again. 'If you don't mind my saying so,' I said, looking at my feet and turning scarlet, 'I don't think it is all right for him. I mean he's dead, isn't he?'

She stopped again, looked me in the eyes and took my hand.

'I'm sorry.'

All the bitterness had drained from her voice. I gazed

at her. I could see why her face changed all the time. It was because her moods changed just as quickly.

'I shouldn't have said that. It's just that I'm stuck here and I don't have anyone my own age to talk to.'

'I should think you could talk to Mr Julian,' said John, as we walked on.

'I'm not sure Mr Julian likes me,' said Rachel.

We reached the gate to the drive, and she said goodbye, turned and walked away from us back to the house. We stood staring at her, but she didn't look round again. Her step was light, and quick, and graceful.

Mr Julian didn't like her? It wasn't possible.

12

It was a fine day, the next Tuesday. The wind had dropped again, and it was one of those golden afternoons of late summer, as we walked past the cornfields to Kelston Lodge.

John was teasing me on the way.

'I've got a surprise for your Mr Julian,' he said. But he wouldn't tell me what it was, although I could see a bulge in his pocket.

Colonel Featherstone met us at the door, and took us round to the terrace, where the tea was already laid out.

Julian was standing stiffly next to a stone statue, wearing a blazer with the left arm tucked into the pocket.

For a moment he caught my eye. He opened his mouth as if he was about to say something, but then his face froze and he looked down.

I stopped where I was, and reddened. But John went straight over to him with a big grin on his face. There was something about John – when he was like that, no one could resist him. Julian's face relaxed and he smiled back.

'How's the leg?' he asked, taking John's hand and shaking it warmly.

'Leg's fine, thanks to you,' said John.

'Do help yourselves to tea,' said Mrs Featherstone.

So we did. We sat on a bench and Mrs Featherstone talked and the Colonel smiled at us, and we kept eating. There were crumpets and raspberry jam, and scones with clotted cream, and a huge fruit cake, and fresh milk. There might have been a war on, but you'd never have known it sitting there by a lawn tennis court, with birds singing all around us. Except for Julian's empty sleeve.

'We don't play tennis so much any more,' Mrs Featherstone commented. 'Not since the war started. Harry was a great one for tennis, but I can't seem to interest Julian, though I'm sure he'd be marvellous at it.'

Julian made no comment. He looked at John, but he took no notice of me at all. I thought he must be annoyed with me for coming there, but I tried not to care. I just wanted to see Miss Rachel again, to see whether she was as beautiful as I'd remembered, to see if it was true that Julian didn't like her.

She came at last, flourishing her long skirt as she swept out through the French windows.

'Don't stand up,' she said, flashing a smile at John, who grinned back at her through a mouthful of cake. 'I hope you're having a good tea.'

She took a cup of tea and a scone, and sat down next to us.

'You're going to have to tell us all about your accident, John, because Julian won't. He just says it was nothing.'

John looked at his cake.

'I can't remember much,' he mumbled. 'Sarah was there. She'll tell you.'

He dug me in the ribs and gave me a cheeky look out of the corner of his eye.

So I told them, and once I got started I made sure it was a good story, like the ones I read, full of daring and danger. The Featherstones loved it, but Julian looked away from us, watching the tops of the trees beyond the tennis court.

'How absolutely thrilling,' said Mrs Featherstone when I'd finished. 'Now we know what you get up to on your long walks, Julian. You should take us out there and show us. We could all go for a picnic. Those nesting seagulls! So exciting!'

'The nesting's finished. The chicks are flown, or dead,' said Julian abruptly.

There was an awful silence.

I didn't really understand it. Julian looked round us all, startled by the fierceness in his own voice, blushing, wishing he could undo it.

Rachel stared at Julian, her cheeks flushed and her mouth slightly open, while Colonel Featherstone fiddled with his fork.

Mrs Featherstone stood up.

'I shall play a little piano if no one minds.'

She walked unsteadily across the terrace. I didn't know what was the matter with her, but I supposed it was something to do with Harry. She only remembered us when she got to the French windows, then she looked back and smiled, though it seemed from very far away.

'You two. It's been so lovely having you. Do eat as much as you want. Then run around the garden, and explore. And come and see me before you go, won't you?'

She went inside, and a moment later the piano started. It was Classical music, such as I'd never heard before: sweet harmonies, full of longing.

Colonel Featherstone stood up too.

'My garden calls me,' he said. 'I must not say no.'

He pottered off round the house.

It was quiet, except for birds singing. John was eyeing another piece of fruit cake.

And suddenly I was aware of Julian and Rachel. They were looking at each other, whether in love or enmity I couldn't say, but there was an electric charge between them. They seemed to have forgotten about us.

I tugged John's arm.

'Come on!' I whispered. 'Let's go and explore, like she said.'

He grabbed the bit of cake and ran after me.

'Why did you run off like that?' said John. 'I was just going to show him the puppy.'

'What puppy?'

'My puppy. The one I'm going to give him.'

John's coat had big pockets. One of them was now full of cake, but from the other he pulled out a little dog.

'You had that there all along?'

''Course I did. She likes being in my pocket, this one.'

He fed her a bit of cake.

'He'd like a dog, wouldn't he? Be a friend for him. I bet he's lonely.'

'He's going to marry Miss Rachel,' I said. 'They'll have lots of babies and be happy ever after.'

'Don't be silly!'

'Why not?'

'He's only got one arm, stupid! A beautiful girl like that isn't going to marry a man with one arm. You can't do it properly with one arm.'

'Do what?'

'You know: kissing and all that. The man puts his arms round the girl. Arms, mind you. Not arm.'

'She wouldn't care about that. He's a hero. She loves him.'

'My brother Will says he loves Betty Prettyjohn. But he just wants to get her in a corner and squeeze her tits.'

'John!' I said. 'Stop talking dirty!'

He picked up the puppy and played with it, while we finished off the cake.

We wandered round the gardens. They seemed to go on for ever, with paths that curled through patches of deep shrubbery, huge old trees, boulders – and then sudden open areas of lawn and flowerbeds. Neither of us had ever been anywhere like it before. Gardens for us meant

68

rows of vegetables fighting against the wind and the salt air, not this sculptured landscape.

'Tell you what,' said John after a while. 'This'd be a great place for hide-and-seek.'

It was. I ran off while he shut his eyes and counted, and then I realised that it was almost too good for hide-and-seek. You could hide anywhere, and not be found for months if you didn't want to be, like on the cliffs in June, when you could lie where you liked and the bracken covered you and you became invisible to everything but the kestrels.

I trotted down a path, and then I found the maze.

I went in, of course. You had to. The little gravel path through tight-clipped box hedges called you in. It can't have been a very big maze, but all the same I was soon lost, so I thought I'd get out again by pushing through the hedge.

It was easy. I just slid in. Behind the leaves the hedge was almost hollow. I came through onto another path, and slid into the next hedge. I was wondering whether I was going out of the maze or further in, when I heard a noise. So I crept along inside the hedge a little way, towards it. Then I stopped, hardly daring to breathe.

I should have jumped out immediately. I know that would have been the right thing to do. Or else slipped silently back the way I'd come. But I didn't, and once I hadn't, I had to stay there, watching something I had no right to witness.

By accident I had come to the centre of the maze.

There was a paved square, and a bench that caught the evening sunlight. On it sat Julian, and in front of him, gazing up at him, knelt Rachel.

In the house, Mrs Featherstone was still playing the piano. The sound came and went, blown in patches on the wind.

13

They were speaking softly, but I was so close I could hear everything.

'You know I can't,' said Julian.

'You can. You can. Of course you can.'

'If only you knew...'

'Then tell me,' said Rachel.

'Your life is whole. I'm different. I can never be whole again.'

'Don't you like me? Not even a little bit?'

'Of course I do. I mean, who wouldn't? I mean, you are the loveliest girl I've ever set eyes on. But you must see that I can't...'

'Why not?'

'You're Harry's sister, for a start.'

'And that should bind us together, shouldn't it? Not keep us apart. You were the last person to see Harry, alive or dead. Doesn't that...'

She broke off. She had seen something in his expression.

'Do you see him in me?' she asked softly.

He nodded.

'What you told my parents about the expression of joy on his face when you found him... You had to say it, didn't you? It was what they wanted to hear. It wasn't true, was it?'

Julian put his hand over his face, and breathed deeply.

'Yes,' he said at last. 'Yes, he died joyfully. It was true.'

Suddenly Rachel buried her head in his knees. Her black hair was loose and hung down around his legs.

'You men,' she said. 'You don't know what we go through. You are out there fighting, being heroes, to live or die by the moment, but we women, we just stay here, stuck, waiting for the bad news. And now Harry's dead, and I'll be here for ever.'

Hesitantly, Julian stretched his hand to her head and touched her hair, but gingerly, as if he was afraid of it.

'The war will be over soon. I should think the young men will be queuing up for you then.'

She tilted her head back suddenly, and looked up at him fiercely.

'It's you I want,' she said. 'Don't you see? You! You! You! I want you to hold me. I want you to kiss me. I want you to love me and marry me and take me away from here to London, or anywhere, for ever.'

Their eyes were locked together. The silence almost crackled. Julian's head began to move forward and Rachel's eyes half shut, and she lifted her face towards him.

Then suddenly he twisted out and stood up.

'I can't,' he said.

She still knelt in front of the seat where he had been a moment before. Her hair hung loose around her face, and the tears swelled in her eyes.

'Don't you understand?' said Julian. 'I have no future. Look!'

With a sudden violence he tore off his blazer, and unbuttoned his shirt, showing the stump of his arm, strangely tailing off from his strong shoulder, with the livid red scars at the end of it.

She turned and looked at him.

He waved the stump about to show her.

'That's what I am. That's what you'd be marrying. A man with a stump for an arm. A cripple. An object of pity. They keep us out of the parades you know, us amputees, because they don't want to frighten the public. My arm lies in bits on the fields of Flanders, eaten by crows. There's a doctor in London who says he can fit a prosthesis, so that I'll be able to hold things, even pick them up. Do you know what a prosthesis is? It's a hook! A glorified hook! Do you really want to marry a man with a hook for a hand? No, no, no, I've got nothing to offer. I can't even work. Nothing. Just empty life stretching ahead of me . . . '

He turned his back on her, and looked up at the top of the hedge where a couple of chaffinches were fluttering.

'You can't fly an aeroplane with one arm, you know. No more the intrepid Birdman. Ever since I can remember that's all I've lived for, all I've ever wanted to do. I can still watch the birds but I can't be one, ever again. I have nothing to live for now.'

The bitterness had all gone from his voice suddenly, and it was just sadness, and as if he was talking to himself.

'Even if you didn't mind the arm, I couldn't have a wife I couldn't support. There's nothing left for me, so I can't offer anything to you. I wish I could have died out in France, like Harry, like the Germans I shot down. I deserved to. I killed and never thought about it, just like everyone else. I'm damaged goods, Rachel. I'm sorry I kept coming back here. It was because of you partly. And partly the birds, and the peace on the cliffs, and the memory of Harry. But it's impossible. It's just impossible...'

Rachel had stood up. She came softly behind him, and touched his shoulder. He turned towards her and they stood silently facing each other. But she wasn't looking at his face, she was looking at the stump of his arm. She reached out and touched it, then fondled it with both her hands. And then she brushed it with her lips.

Julian shut his eyes, and an expression that might have been agony or joy, or a mixture of both, came over his face. His good arm surrounded her and tugged her close to him.

And then they kissed.

I shouldn't have watched, but I couldn't take my eyes away. I'd never seen a kiss before. He folded his lips around hers and it looked as if his tongue went right into her mouth. It was exciting and disgusting at the same time.

She sank to her knees, and he came down with her, without separating their lips, as if they were glued together at the mouth. And a moment later they were rolling together on the paved floor that was dappled by the evening sun. Julian was squeezing Rachel's waist, pulling her as close as she could get, and she had her arms twined round his neck, kissing him passionately on the mouth, the neck, the eyes – all over his face.

Then, quite suddenly, he broke away.

A contortion went through his body, and it was as if he tore himself from her. She sat up amazed. There were spots of moss on her white dress.

'I can't,' he said. 'I wish I could, but I can't. I'm sorry. I'm so sorry. I shouldn't have come here.'

He looked at her, his eyes big with emotion.

'I have to move on, Rachel. It's the only way. You bring back too many memories. I do love you. But I wouldn't make you happy.'

'I thought you were a hero,' said Rachel in a voice that was soft but deadly. 'You're not. You're a coward.'

'Yes,' said Julian. 'I am. I am.'

He grabbed his jacket and ran out of the maze. A moment later he passed me on the other side of the hedge. I thought: I hope he knows his way out.

Miss Rachel sat there on the ground, and the sun lit up her tousled hair. Her cheeks were flushed, and her eyes were moist, and I thought she was going to cry. But she didn't. She just sat there for an age, and then she let out a deep sigh, stood up, brushed the dirt from her dress, and walked away.

14

I was looking for John, but I couldn't find him. And then I saw Julian, sitting on a bench by a flowerbed, slumped forward with his head in his hand.

I nearly slipped back into the bushes. But he looked so sad and lonely. I felt so sorry for him.

I went and sat beside him. He took no notice of me. The evening sun was lighting up the flowers and they looked very pretty.

'Why won't you speak to me?' I said at last. 'Have I done something wrong?'

He looked up, and seemed to take me in for the first time that day.

'No, no. Nothing wrong. It's just – I didn't expect you here. I mean, we're from different worlds. You wouldn't understand.'

He put his head back in his hand. He seemed to have forgotten me again.

'Miss Rachel loves you. I know she does,' I blurted out suddenly.

He looked round at me, shocked.

'What could you possibly know about it?' he said.

He turned his back on me and shut me out. Then he stood up and walked away down the path. I was waiting for him to turn around and look back at me. He didn't have to smile, just show he knew I was there. But he didn't.

All I was for him was a little girl with a pretty face, from the fishing village.

I found John in the end. He was with Colonel Featherstone in the walled garden, looking at the vegetables, and he'd forgotten all about me.

They were in a huge glasshouse, all hung with grapes and peaches.

Colonel Featherstone picked a peach and gave it to me. The flesh was white. It was sweet like nothing I'd ever tasted before.

'I've been showing your friend here our vegetable patch,' said the Colonel, leading us out and gesturing at a great sea of vegetable marrows. 'I hope I can persuade him to come and work for me. We need all the help we can get. Look at those weeds!'

'Are you all right?' said John, looking at me oddly.

'Why shouldn't I be?' I answered sharply. 'We'd better be getting home though.'

Colonel Featherstone looked at his watch.

'My goodness me, doesn't time fly? Where's Julian got to? And Rachel? I'm sure they'd want to say goodbye to you. Let's go and find them.'

Mrs Featherstone was still playing the piano. Julian was on the terrace. John went straight up to him.

'I've got something for you,' he said. 'A present.'

Julian looked up, surprised. John took the puppy out of his pocket, and held it out to him.

'She's the best of the litter. She'd be a good friend

to you.'

Julian reached out his big hand and took the little puppy in it. He put her on his lap and stroked her, and she went quiet and looked up at him.

'Man's best friend,' said John.

'Yes,' said Julian. 'Yes indeed. How did you know I like dogs?'

He gazed down into her face and she reached her tongue out and tried to lick him.

'But she's too young to be parted from her mother.'

'I'll bring her over again in a few weeks. She'll be ready then,' said John.

'No,' said Julian. 'I'm leaving tonight, for a while. But I'll come and fetch her when I'm back. That'll be better.'

He picked up the little dog and held her very close to his nose. She wagged her tail and tried to lick him.

'I'll call her Beauty. She really is one.'

He handed her back to John.

'Look after her well for me.'

'Mind you do come for her though,' said John. 'You won't forget?'

'I won't forget.'

We couldn't find Miss Rachel, but Mrs Featherstone stopped her playing and came out and shook our hands with a faraway look in her eyes, as if she'd forgotten about us already.

'Lovely to have you. Do come again!'

Then she went back to the piano.

Colonel Featherstone walked us down the drive, showing us the shrubs, telling us how this one came from India, that one from Africa, picking out individual trees and praising their splendour or the beauty of their trunks.

John listened to it all, but it passed over the top of my head.

'Not a bad old bloke,' said John, when he'd left us on the road. 'Says he'll pay me a shilling a day if I come and work there, do a bit of weeding and that. That's not bad – a shilling a day.'

'John,' I said. 'Do you think if two people are in love they ought to marry, no matter what?'

'You mean like if they're not suited or something?'

'Something like that.'

John thought for a while.

'No,' he said at last. 'You've got to be suited.'

We walked on in silence till we came to the top of the hill. Hallsands was below us, looking as if it was perched on top of the sea, and already in deep shade. Behind us the sun was setting behind the moors, in a splash of purple.

We stopped for a moment.

'John,' I said. 'Would you like to kiss me?'

'What?'

'Go on! Kiss me! Kiss me proper! On the lips! You can put your tongue in my mouth, if you like.'

'Don't be daft,' said John.

15

The days are drawing in, but it's still fine and the sun sets orange across the bay. Sarah's baby is due very soon now, but she hasn't forgotten about me. She came over today and took me to see my old friend, John Mingo.

We drove past Kelston Grange. Its gardens are famous now, and open to the public three days a week in the summer. But different people live there, people I don't know.

In Kelston village I made Sarah stop.

'I just want to look at the church,' I said.

Sarah took Judy for a walk, and I sat on a seat in Kelston churchyard, where I could see the big oak tree behind the church, and remembered.

I must have been fourteen or fifteen. The war was over, I'm sure of that. John was there, in his best clothes. We stood in the churchyard watching the gentry drive up so smart in their cars and carriages. But Colonel Featherstone had the church doors left open so that we could hear the organ music, join in the hymns, catch snatched phrases from the service.

'Do you, Rachel Lydia, take this man to be your lawful wedded husband?'

'I do.'

At last Miss Rachel came out. She was dressed in white satin with her veil pushed back and a train stretching behind her. I'd never seen her so beautiful.

'Kiss the bride!' somebody shouted. Everybody cheered.

Except for me. I turned and ran off on my own, with bitter tears . . .

Sarah drove me on to Kingsbridge, to John's nursing home.

What a smart place! It was one of the grand houses of the area once, and it still looks impressive, with all those windows and turrets. Quite a contrast to our old cottages in Hallsands.

'Well, you've come up in the world, haven't you?' I said when I saw him.

'By golly!' he said. 'It's little Sarah, isn't it?'

'Little yourself!' I said. But he's still a big man, and he'd tower over me if he could stand.

'What are you doing still alive?' said John. 'Come and sit down here where I can see you better.'

We were in the lounge. Some of the other residents smiled at me, and nodded. Others were lost in worlds of their own. You have to watch out for that when you're old – the past swirling up and sucking you away in it.

That's not John's problem though. He's gone in the legs and his eyes are dim, but inside he's the same old John, the same boy I played with over eighty years ago.

'You're looking beautiful,' he said, as I sat down in a

high-backed chair next to him.

'You don't look too bad yourself.'

'I didn't know you were still alive. I'll tell you what. We're the last two.'

'The last two what?'

'The last two from Hallsands. The last two that ever lived there. The last two that remember it as something real, not just a story.'

He paused while we both thought about that.

'It was real, wasn't it? We were children there. We went fishing . . .'

'And you went after gulls' eggs.'

'O aye, I went after gulls' eggs all right.'

He chuckled, and disappeared for a bit back into his memories. Then he leaned over and took my hand.

'It's good to see you, Sarah. There's nothing like someone from the old times. Do you remember when we were walking back from the Grange, and you asked me to kiss you?'

'I certainly do,' I said.

'Well that's my one regret in life,' he said. 'I always wished I'd said yes.'

'It's not too late, John Mingo,' I said. 'You can do it now if you like.'

'Can I?' he said.

I stood up and bent over him. He put his hands up to my face and pulled me down, and gave me a big, long, cheeky kiss, full on the lips.

For a moment the world went silent and I didn't know

where I was, who I was, certainly not what age I was. And then I came back, and the other old people, those that had their wits, were all laughing and clapping.

I hugged John, for a last time. Then I left before it got too much for both of us.

16

Winter came suddenly, with hail pocking the sea. The wind moved from west to north, and then veered to the east.

I lit a coal fire every day in the parlour, and the house was snug, but it felt empty. My brothers had gone. They went to Plymouth and both signed up for the Royal Navy. Trevor had to lie about his age, but they were only too willing to believe him.

My mother said nothing about it. That was the worst of it. She went on running the post office, which wasn't much work for such a small village, and cleaned and tidied and polished as ever. But in between, she sat in her chair by the fire and sewed or stared into space, and didn't even bother to scold me any more.

The neighbours came in and asked her how she was.

'I'm fine,' she'd say. ' Why shouldn't I be?'

But she never left the house. Whatever had to be done outside, I did. I fetched the water, and did the shopping, and ran errands. I'd try to get her to come out, but with no success.

'Come and have a look, Mam,' I'd coax her. 'The Trouts have got a huge catch this morning. There's lobsters and all.'

She'd shake her head and purse her lips.

'I don't want to see the sea,' she'd say. 'I don't like it.'

But she couldn't escape hearing its voice. The gentle slushing on the beach in calm weather, and the roar of the waves in a storm, and the endless mewing of the seagulls.

John went and worked for Colonel Featherstone on Saturdays, coming back proudly with his shilling. On Sunday mornings I sat with the Mingos in chapel; my mother hadn't been since my father died, because she wouldn't leave the house, but she still wanted me to go. Then afterwards I'd sit with John on the sea wall, and suck toffees, and hear the news about the Featherstones.

Skip and her puppy, Beauty, scavenged along the foreshore, never far away. The puppy was turning into a fine little dog, very bright and inquisitive.

'I'm still keeping her for Mr Julian,' said John. 'He hasn't been back to the Grange since we went to tea that day, but I reckon he will be soon. He promised to have her, didn't he? He'd keep his promise, someone like that.'

'I reckon,' I said. But I didn't want to talk about him. 'Do you see Miss Rachel?'

John grinned.

'Don't you worry about her. She knows how to get what she wants, Miss Rachel does. She comes and talks to me while I'm weeding. We have a laugh together when she's not moaning about something. She'll marry a rich man one of these days, and boss him out of his socks!'

No she won't, I thought. She'll marry Julian and they'll be happy. And then I pushed the thought away.

We watched the storm clouds gathering, out beyond the bay: great black cumulus clouds over a slatey sea. A thin sun lit up the shingle of the beach. Our beach. Still there, for all Mr Mingo's warnings. It had even grown bigger that autumn as the tide washed in sand.

'My dad says there'll be a big storm tonight,' said John. 'He says the sea might come over the wall.'

It didn't seem likely. We were sitting on the wall and it was high and solid.

'Our house'll be all right anyway,' I said. 'It's the houses on the sea side that get the worst of it.'

Later we helped pull the boats up the slipway onto the wall. Evening was coming on, and the clouds were tinged yellow. It was strangely still. Not a breath of wind. Just this yellow light of the setting sun reflected off the black clouds.

But the sea warned us of the coming storm. As long as the wind was in the west our bay was always calm, even in rough weather, but now a huge swell from the east was crashing straight against the beach, and raising plumes of spray on the cliffs. It was low tide, though, and the beach with its millions of little round pebbles seemed a comfortable buffer against the force of the sea.

We pulled the boats right up into the street, and everyone lent a hand. As we worked, the wind came in a sudden gust that blew spray into our faces.

Mr Mingo looked out to sea, anxiously.

'High tide is just past midnight,' he said. 'If the wall still stands then, I reckon we're safe. For now.'

Before I went inside, I had a look at my little garden, sheltered behind the house. The thrift and the primroses had died back, but it still looked pretty. I pulled away some dead leaves and rearranged the pebbles where a cat had disturbed them. I gave my special green stone a little polish.

As I went round to the front of the house, the wind nearly took me off my feet.

It was cosy inside, with a coal fire glowing. My mother had lit the oil lamp, and I lit a candle for myself. We had a supper of fish pie and potatoes and cabbage, and a glass of milk. It was plain food, but it was fresh and tasty.

'Mr Mingo says it'll be a big storm tonight,' I said.

'Aye,' said my mother.

'He says we should watch out the sea don't break down the wall and drown us all.'

'Aye,' said my mother. 'Is there enough salt on your potatoes?'

'Mr Mingo says we should get ready to leave quickly if we have to, if the worst comes to the worst.'

My mother pursed her lips.

'Not me,' she said. 'I'll be safer here, thank you. It's clean and tidy here. It's nice, isn't it, Sarah?'

I looked around. Whatever else, she had the house

perfect. Everything was in its place: the best china on the dresser; the framed photo of my father in his navy uniform; the clock on the mantelpiece, polished so that you could see your face in the brass; the scrubbed oak table where I ate and read and did my homework...

It was more than nice. It was lovely.

We washed the dishes together, using hot water from the kettle that lived over the fire, and using it sparingly because all the water had to be fetched from the well. Then she turned up the lamp so that she could see to sew, and I read a book about Captain Cook, that my teacher had lent me.

You remember those little things, when your life is about to change for ever.

Outside the wind was working up a fury. It whistled and buffeted round the house. It gusted down the chimney and filled the room with coal smoke, making us cough.

'Better close down the fire and go to bed,' said my mother, drawing her shawl about her.

I made a plaster of damp ash and covered the fire with it, to keep it in overnight. Then I went into the kitchen that was also our bathroom, and washed my hands and face.

'Goodnight, Mam!'

'Goodnight, Sarah!'

I opened the door that led to the stairs. My candle flickered in the draught. I lingered there, because I didn't want to leave the safety of our sitting room for the cold and dark of my bedroom, with the wind howling about it. It felt spooky since my brothers had left.

'Get on with you now!'

My mother looked up and smiled at me. It was a rare thing for her to smile in those days, and it reassured me.

I lay in my bed with all the blankets pulled up round my head, listening to the wind and the waves, until they turned to a strange music, in which I heard aeroplanes banking and turning, and the roar of distant guns from the Front, and the cries of seabirds, and Mrs Featherstone's piano, and voices talking and singing and laughing and crying. All mixed up together, as I drifted in and out of sleep...

I was woken by a crash.

I sat up in bed, rigid.

'Sarah!' my mother shouted from downstairs. I grabbed my clothes from under my pillow and felt my way to the door, then tumbled downstairs to the kitchen.

My mother was lighting the storm lamp. It flared up as the wick caught, deepening the wrinkles on her face.

I dressed and put on my coat. We could see the street through the window. There were lights waving in the darkness, and figures struggling against the storm.

'Go and see what's happened, Sarah,' said my mother. 'Don't be long. Come straight back and tell me.'

I took the storm lantern, and opened the door.

17

I was hit by the wind and a shower of foam. I struggled to pull the door shut behind me and keep the lantern steady.

The street was full of people shouting, and lanterns swinging, and gusts of foam as the waves broke.

Mrs Stokes, our neighbour, came beside me and took my arm. We pushed our way through the wind, down the street to the sea wall.

The sky was not all black. From time to time a half moon flashed out behind the racing clouds. It lit up Mr Fawkes' house. Or what was left of it.

It was a terrible sight. Mr Fawkes' house was one of the nicest in the village, I thought: a thatched cottage with a view over the bay. But it was built over a crack in the rock platform, that had filled up with sand thousands of years ago.

The wall held back the sand. And the wall was broken. The sea had sucked the sand from behind it, leaving a chasm three yards across and ten foot deep. The waves were churning through it.

The sides of the house still stood. The coal still glowed in the fireplace. But between them there was nothing but rubble: stone and plaster and thatch, and broken bits of furniture, already being sucked away by the sea.

I could see Mr Fawkes and his old wife on the other side of the chasm, standing among a little crowd, lit by storm lanterns. Mrs Mingo put a blanket round them.

John was there too, holding a lantern.

But there was a gaping hole between us and no way across. Even our shouts were drowned by the roar of the sea.

At that moment another wave burst against what was left of the sea wall, and the water rose up in a huge fan, sparkling in the moonlight. Mrs Stokes pulled me back to the shelter of the houses, and the water landed in the road to flow back through the widening chasm.

'Go back home, now!' shouted Mrs Stokes, against the gale. 'You and your mam, pack your things! We'll all get out of here at low tide in the morning.'

It was a relief to close the door behind me, to keep out some of the noise of wind and waves.

The clock was still ticking on the mantelpiece. I glanced at it as I came back in. It said 11.45. It was nearly high tide.

'Well?' asked my mam.

'Mr Fawkes' house has gone,' I said.

She shook her head.

'They shouldn't have built there in the first place. Don't build your house on sand. It says so in the Bible.'

'The sea's broken the wall,' I said. 'I've never seen it like this before, Mam. I think the beach has gone. I think the sea's going to take everything! Mrs Stokes says we should pack up ready to leave in the morning.'

My mother pursed her lips, went to the window and closed the shutters.

'We'll see about that. Go back to bed now,' she said.

I didn't want to leave the warmth of the sitting room, but I went. I crept up the dark stairs without even a candle. The wind was whistling through the eaves and my bedroom window was rattling. Outside I could hear the crash of the waves breaking against the houses on the sea side.

But my bed was still warm. It was my own bed, where I'd always slept, safe and familiar. How often I'd lain there listening to storms and feeling snug in my blankets! The tide would soon be turning, and perhaps if I lay very quiet, the storm would quieten too. I pulled the blankets over my head, and shut my eyes.

The wave hit us.

My window smashed. Pebbles and broken glass washed across the bedroom floor, in a gush of seawater.

The wind was roaring through the room, scattering my school books.

And then the roof started to go – a sheaf of thatch pulled away as if by a giant hand, and a patch of black beyond the rafters.

I grabbed my blankets and ran downstairs.

'The sea broke the window, Mam! The roof's going!'

My mother was standing in front of the fire, her face a mask of tension. She grabbed me and held me close.

Another wave broke. There was a crash and a whoosh of foam. The door buckled, and we heard the glass smashing in the front window.

Then there was water coming down the stairs, oozing through the shutters and under the door, ruining my mother's carpet.

We stood there, and let it wash round our ankles. The candles had blown out, but the storm lamp was still burning, and the fire glowed.

Slowly, the sea drained away under the door, back into the street. We just watched it. There was nothing else we could do.

The next wave broke. Again the door buckled under the weight of water, but held.

This time water came splashing down the chimney, making the fire hiss and steam.

We went on standing, too scared to move, waiting for the big one that would knock down the door, and break the front wall, and collapse the ceiling, and suck us away with it.

But the next wave was smaller. This time only foam and shingle spattered across the front of the house. And the next one too. And the one after... Even the wind seemed to have dropped a bit...

Suddenly there was a hammering on the door. I slid open the bolt, and in rushed Mr Stokes, with Mr Login behind him.

'How's your house?' he asked.

93

My mother said nothing.

'The roof's off, and the sea came in upstairs,' I said.

'Then you're better off than most! The houses on the sea front are all gone. We're lucky to be alive. We can't get down the street to the other end of the village, so we have to wait for the tide. Can you take a few in?'

I nodded, and shut the door behind them as they hurried out.

My mother was still standing, looking straight ahead, as if she couldn't bear to see what was happening all around us. I led her to her chair. Then she saw the clock, untouched and shining as ever on the mantelpiece. She stroked it with her fingertips, then she picked it up.

'It's still going,' she said. 'The clock's still ticking.'

'Sit there, Mam,' I said. She sat with the clock on her knee, stroking it as if it was a little dog.

Mr Stokes came back with Mrs Login and her baby and three little children. The children were bedraggled and confused, still half asleep. I gave them a blanket each, and they settled down on the table, which was the driest place.

Mrs Login and I tried to get the fire going. We managed it in the end. It steamed at first, and then it smoked, but it warmed us. We even made a cup of tea. You get through the bad times better if you keep busy.

Mrs Login had left her house moments before the waves wrecked it. She'd seen her furniture, her pictures, all her precious things, smashed up by the sea. But she was a sensible body. She wasn't thinking about that. She was thinking about keeping her children warm, and feeding her baby.

The storm raged on. Every few minutes, foam spattered the shutters, and once or twice a lick of water came under the front door. But the immediate danger was over. The tide had turned.

I didn't dare go upstairs and see what was left of our bedrooms. I couldn't have left the warmth, and the company.

Mrs Login glanced sometimes at my mother, but my mother didn't look at anybody or say anything. She drank her tea, and then she closed her eyes.

Perhaps she was asleep, but I doubt it.

The night was long and full of noises. The village was falling down around us. There was a chasm in the road that we couldn't cross, and no way up the cliff behind us. I wished John were with us. Or Mr Mingo. He'd know what to do.

'Wait for the morning,' said Mrs Login, trying her hardest to be cheerful. 'It'll be better in the daylight.'

I doubted it.

18

Perhaps I did sleep in the end. At any rate I opened my eyes to see Mr Login at the door and a dim light of dawn behind him.

'Move yourselves!' he said urgently. 'The tide's out. We can get along the foreshore if we're quick.'

Mrs Login bundled her children off the table and out into the street, holding onto them tight to stop the wind from blowing them away.

Mr Login glanced at my mother, who still had her eyes closed. Then he turned to me.

'We haven't got long, girl. Get your mother out. There'll not be a lot of this house left after the next high tide.'

He shut the door as he went.

'Mam!' I shouted. 'Mam!'

I shook her and she opened her eyes.

'Mam, we've got to go.'

She blinked and looked around, as if waking up.

'What a mess! We'd better get cleaning up.'

'Mam, the sea'll be back soon. The house is done for. We've got to go.'

She seemed to understand, but she shook her head. Then she took my hand.

'You go. I've got to clean up here. I can't leave it in this mess.'

'Mam, please!'

She stood up and put the clock back on the mantelpiece. Then she wiped my father's photograph with her handkerchief.

'You go now,' she said. 'Don't worry about me.'

The door burst open again. This time it was Mr Stokes. He had a sackful of his possessions over his shoulder.

'Take what you can carry, and get out now!' he shouted. 'The tide's turning and the beach has gone. We can't wait.'

He left the door open, and the cold wind blew in around us. I could see dim figures in the half light hurrying down the street to the shore. The village was emptying.

'Shut that door,' said my mother. 'I don't like the draught.'

I tore at her skirts, trying to pull her out.

'Mam! Mam!' I pleaded.

She looked down at me. At last I felt that she was there, that she was taking me in.

'Run after Mr Stokes now, Sarah. He'll take you over. Then find the Mingos. They'll look after you. I'll come later, when I've cleared up.'

'There won't be a later, Mam,' I cried. 'The roof's gone. You'll die if you stay here. You've got to come. You've got to.'

She hesitated.

'They always say that when there's a storm,' she said.

'No, Mam, it's for real this time. You should see it out there.'

She took a step towards the door, but instead of going out she pushed it shut. Then she turned back to me.

'Go upstairs and get my box. It's under my bed.'

I ran up the stairs. Most of the roof was off now, and I picked my way through broken beams and sodden thatch to where her bedroom was, at the back of the house. It was quieter here, and the roof still held over her bed. I knew what box she meant, and it was still there, though I didn't know then what was in it. I tucked it under my arm.

I passed back through the remains of my bedroom on the way to the stairs, and paused there. The roof was off and the wind gusted through the rafters.

I looked around in the dawn light. My little bedside table had tipped over, spilling the contents of its drawer. The book I'd been reading was upside down and open on the floor. I picked it up. It wasn't mine and I had to return it. I didn't even look at the rest of my things. I didn't want them.

Then I noticed the paper aeroplane. The one the Birdman had made for me, on the cliffs, what seemed an age ago. Somehow it had arrived on my bed, and it sat there looking as if it might take off at any moment and fly us all away.

I took it, and folded it into the book for safety.

Then I went downstairs.

'Here it is, Mam!'

She took her box from me, and opened the front door. The wind, laced with spray, blasted through at us.

It was too much for her. She looked desperately round and took a step back towards me. All the colour drained from her face, and she collapsed, still clutching her box.

'Mam!'

I bent over her.

'Mam! Wake up!'

She was still breathing. She'd only fainted. She opened her eyes and looked at me.

'You go, Sarah,' she whispered. 'I can't go out there. You go. I'll be all right.'

'I'll get help, Mam. I'll be back,' I said, and ran out into the street.

Almost everyone had already gone. A few last stragglers were hurrying towards the shore. Around me was desolation.

Our house was one of the better ones, with half the roof still on, and none of the walls down. The Logins' house, which had taken the full brunt of the sea, had one wall standing. The house next to it had its front intact and perfect, but the side walls and the roof had fallen in. Everywhere was sprayed with shingle – the remains of our beach, which the sea had sucked up and spat back at us.

Most of the sea wall had held, or surely we would all have been washed away. People were climbing over it, down to the shore – the only way out now that the street was broken.

I stopped at the wall and looked over.

There was the sea. The raging sea, grey in the dawn

light, with wild splashes of white foam as mountainous wave after wave crashed in towards us.

I'd seen it often enough, though never quite as furious as now.

But where was our beach? Where was the mighty ridge of shingle where we played, and mended nets, and beached the boats, and admired the catches, and primed the crab pots with pilchard?

All that was left of it was a thin covering of pebbles on a sloping rock bed, ten foot below me.

And the sea was terribly near, although it was low tide. The massive waves thundered against the rock our village was built on, with nothing to break their power.

I half slid down from the wall, wondering how the old people and the little children had managed it. Then I ran the hundred yards across the rock to the slipway, where the path led up to the clifftop and safety.

It was crowded. Children were crying, old people were looking dazed. Those who had the strength were pulling furniture and valuables from the wreckage of their homes, and struggling with it up the cliff path.

There were strangers there too, people from the neighbourhood who'd heard of or guessed our plight, and come to help.

At last I saw John, talking to a man. Skip was at his heels, and he was holding Beauty.

It was such a relief to see him. I ran up to him.

'John!' I shouted. 'John! Where's your dad?'

The man he was talking to turned at the sound of my voice, so I saw his face.

It was Julian.

I stopped. I couldn't say anything. I felt I was choking. A great surge of emotion was pulsing through me, that I didn't want or understand. Ever since I'd last seen him, I'd tried not to think about Julian, but he kept coming back into my head. I couldn't forget his stories of the war, nor how he'd kissed Rachel. But I couldn't forget how he'd turned away and shut me out either. And now he was here in front me, and I felt a rage of resentment against him. As if he'd betrayed me doubly by coming back at this of all times.

'What's up, Sarah?' asked John, alarmed.

'Can I help?' said Julian.

'No you can't!' I glared at him. 'What are you doing here anyway? Come to gawp at us I suppose...'

'I... I thought I could help,' said Julian, taken aback.

'Fat lot of help you'd be, with your one arm and your self-pity.'

I almost screamed it at him. I didn't know why I was saying it, even at the time. It wasn't like me, and it wasn't what I really thought either. I just couldn't bear for him to see the wreck of our lives.

I looked at the little dog that John was holding.

'Come to get your dog, have you? Thought you might miss your chance?'

I couldn't stop myself. All my fears, griefs,

resentments were landing on him.

'It wasn't like that,' he said. 'I heard what was happening, and I just came at once. It was you and John I was worried about...'

I burst into tears. John dropped the dog and put an arm around me.

'What's going on, Sarah?' he asked.

'It's my mam,' I sobbed. ' She wouldn't come out and now she's fallen. She's going to die, John, she's going to die.'

John was looking over my shoulder and saw his brother.

'Tom!' he shouted. 'Find Dad! Tell him to go to Mrs Coleman's, now.'

He stood back and gripped my shoulders.

'Pull yourself together, Sarah! We'll get her out. Let's get back over.'

He looked at Julian.

'Don't take any notice of what she says. She don't mean it. Come on!'

I gulped back my tears. My anger was fading already, and I knew that John was right.

I glanced at Julian and muttered, 'Sorry,' but I don't think he heard. He didn't look upset, though. He looked determined.

The three of us ran back along the shore, the dogs following us.

The sea had already risen. The cresting waves towered up a few yards from us, and the water splashed around our feet. The tide was coming in, but how fast, I couldn't tell without the beach.

Nothing was as it should be any more.

Our end of the village was deserted now. You couldn't say it was quiet, with the roar of the wind and the sea, but behind that roar was the stillness of a ghost town. There was just one sign of life – the smoke from our chimney.

My mother was sitting on her chair. She seemed better. She'd even built up the fire and it was warm in the little room.

She looked up when we came in.

'I think I'll stay here now, Sarah,' she said. 'The storm's past its worst. I don't want those dogs in the house, mind,' she added, looking disapprovingly at Skip and Beauty who were nosing their way in.

We shut the door, and the dogs whimpered behind it.

'Come on, Mrs Coleman,' said John. 'The tide's coming in again. We'll help you. We'll bring your clock and your pictures and everything.'

'You're a good boy, John,' said my mother. But she made no move to get up.

'We've got to go, Mam...' I was saying, but Julian stepped past me. If he was still upset from what I'd said to him, he didn't show it.

'Please let us help you, Mrs Coleman. Because the sea's coming back, and it won't spare this house a second time. So please come with us. For your daughter's sake.'

She shook her head.

'We won't go without you, Mrs Coleman,' said John.

'We don't have much time,' said Julian. 'What would you like us to take? We should pack it up now.'

'I'm not going,' said my mother.

Julian knelt down beside her. He spoke softly in his clipped upper-class voice.

'You have to go now,' he said. 'There's no roof on your house any more. It's only a matter of time before the ceiling and the walls go, and the sea flows through it. Everyone else has left. Come with us, please. It's our last chance.'

'I'll be all right here,' she said. 'Don't you worry about me.'

We looked at each other. We really didn't know what to do.

'You two go back,' I said. 'I'll stay with her. We'll stick it out till the next low tide.'

'No,' said Julian. 'You go. I'll stay.'

'ALICE!'

We turned. The big frame of Mr Mingo filled the doorway.

'What are you making so much trouble for, Alice? As if there wasn't enough already. Get your things now. We're going.'

She looked up at him.

'I can't do it, Jack,' she said. 'I can't go out there.'

He took the photo of my father off the wall, and held it in front of her.

'Think of Ted. He would not have wanted you to leave his girl an orphan now, would he?'

My mother hesitated.

'I cannot look at the sea, Jack.'

'Neither you will, Alice,' said Mr Mingo softly. 'You'll come with us, and you'll keep your eyes closed, and your shawl round your head, and we'll guide you. John, take her box. You sir, can you carry the clock? Sarah, you know what's precious to her, pick it up and bring it, as fast as you can.'

And before my mother could argue, he took her arm and led her to the door and out through it, into the gale.

I was the last to leave. I packed a few oddments in a basket – her best hat which she never wore, the milk jug, and the brass dogs from in front of the fire. My book, of course. And the paper aeroplane.

Then, on an urge, I ran round the back of the house to say goodbye to my little garden.

I don't know what I expected to see. Chaos, probably. But by some miracle it was still there. The pebbles were swept by wind and foam, but the pattern was still recognisable. I straightened it a little. Then I picked up the green stone and slipped it in my pocket.

As I came back in front of the house I noticed our front door was swinging in the gale. My mam never liked the door open. I pulled it to, although there didn't seem much point: the sea would make short work of it.

I ran after the others.

19

'The sea's too high,' said Mr Mingo. 'We daren't risk it. One big wave and we're drowned.'

He was standing by the wall, looking at the vast breakers crashing down in front of us. He shook his head, and led us on down the street, till we reached the cleft where Mr Fawkes' house had been.

The waves were churning through it, making that sucking noise you hear in sea-caves.

'Wait here!' he commanded.

I held my mother's arm, and she drew her shawl tighter around her face, while Mr Mingo and Julian pulled a long timber from the roof of a shattered house. John helped them lay it across the chasm. They pulled out another one and made a fragile bridge.

'You go first!' said Mr Mingo.

I crossed, not looking down, and my mother followed. I thought she'd refuse, but she stepped nimbly enough, opening her shawl just enough to see where she trod. Her resistance had gone.

We waited on the other side. John came next, then Julian. Mr Mingo was last. He was the heaviest of us, and as he reached the centre, one of the timbers cracked. He caught his balance in time, and jumped to safety.

Then I remembered.

'The dogs!' I said. 'Where are the dogs?'

'They stayed with you,' said John.

'They didn't!' I said, and at that moment I realised what had happened. The dogs were always trying to get into our house, and when my mother left, no one was there to stop them. They'd finally managed it...

'They're shut in the house. Oh Lord, I shut them in when I left.'

I was going to run back over, but Julian was ahead of me, and Mr Mingo put a hand on my shoulder to hold me back. My mother was clinging to me too.

Julian half ran across the one remaining timber, and disappeared up the street.

We waited, the sea churning in the chasm, and the spray splashing our faces with each successive wave.

At last the dogs came, barking and nipping each other with the joy of being free. They hesitated at the timber bridge, but saw there was no choice and trotted sure-footedly over. John crouched down and they jumped up at him, licking his face.

Julian followed. He steadied himself before the bridge, and looked down.

Each wave that roared into the chasm seemed stronger than the last.

He stepped onto the timber. Suddenly I was worried for him. He seemed hesitant now, moving his feet carefully, as if he was thinking too much about it, as if he feared falling.

The timber cracked.

We could hear it over the noise of the sea.

We saw Julian lose his balance, and thrash out wildly with his one arm, trying to save himself.

The timber broke, and he fell. But he caught at the wood with his hand and hung on fiercely. Mr Mingo grabbed the other end of it and threw himself on the ground to get better leverage. Julian was kicking with his feet, trying to get a grip on a rock ledge.

Then the wave came. The biggest yet. It thundered into the chasm, sweeping Julian away with it. Then it pulled back with an equal force. Julian's head and hand emerged briefly from the surf as it sucked him back towards the sea.

It was so strong. He had no hope of a foothold.

There was a net. I saw it in one of those flashes when time loses its force in the face of what is happening. A fishing net, bunched up in the gutter.

I grabbed it, and I threw, as the next wave broke.

And as Julian was thrown back up the chasm again in the force of it, he washed against the net and it caught him.

Mr Mingo was clinging on, from our end. And John. And my mother had thrown down her shawl and was pulling for all she was worth.

The sea went back, and Julian stayed in the net, well tangled, while we hauled him in like a fish.

He lay on the street, with the net still around him.

His eyes were shut. His cheeks were cold and pale in the early morning light.

I thought: The dead are beautiful. And as the others

hesitated, I knelt down beside him and touched his lips.

It was like a miracle – his eyes opened, and he tried to smile. Then the next moment he rolled over, coughing and retching.

I took a step away, as Mr Mingo moved in past me to help him. My mother was standing next to me, waiting quietly.

And then I knew what I had to do.

Julian was alive. That was enough. He would marry Miss Rachel, because they loved each other. And they'd live in a big house and have servants, and babies, and he wouldn't think of me again. That was the way things were. And that was how it should be. There was no place for me in that life. He was in his world, and I was in mine. I had to forget about him.

I had to look after what was mine, now and forever.

I took my mother's arm, and led her on, through the ruined village and up the zigzag path to the coastguard's cottage, which was crowded with women and children seeking refuge. At least it was warm and out of the wind.

Mrs Mingo came up to us and put her arm round my mother, and they sat down together without speaking. Behind us, in the corner, Mrs Login's baby kept crying and crying.

The crying was getting on my nerves.

'I'll go outside, Mam,' I said.

She nodded, and I went back out to the clifftop.

*

The wind hit me with a flurry of hail. I threw myself down and pressed myself into the heather to find some shelter. Then I watched the immensity of the waves. Even up there I could feel the spray on my face. Below me in the village, people still struggled to salvage possessions from the ruins of the houses, and drag them up the path to the safety of the clifftop, where they piled up in clumsy heaps of uncertain destination.

The sky was brightening, with streaks of yellow between the clouds eastward. And the tide was rising. I watched a wall of the London Inn crumble beneath an enormous wave.

And for the first time it really hit me.

It was gone. The whole village. My whole world. And it would never return. I didn't want to cry. I just felt empty.

I sensed someone behind me, and turned to see Julian. His cheek was scratched and his clothes were sodden and filthy. He was carrying his little dog under his arm.

I sat up and faced him.

'I'm going,' he said hesitantly.

'All right,' I said.

'I just wanted to say...how sorry I am...about all this.'

His face was crumpling up like a little child's, but I didn't care.

'There's no point in talking about it,' I said. 'It won't bring it back.'

I turned my back on him and watched the devastation.

The roof of the chapel was caving in.

'Thank you, Sarah,' he said. 'For everything.'

I said nothing. He was still standing there, expecting me to turn back to him, but I wasn't going to.

'Perhaps we'll meet again,' he said hopefully. 'In happier times.'

'I shouldn't think so. We're from different worlds, aren't we? I suppose I might be your servant,' I said, as the backwash of a huge wave sucked away the stables of the London Inn.

And then I was sorry. I wanted to tell him what he meant to me. I wanted to make it all right.

I turned round, but he had already gone.

20

But we did meet again, after all.

There was sunshine and birdsong, and a warm, gentle breeze. The organ music flowed triumphantly through the open doors of the church. I was in my best dress and John in his new smart suit. The war was over, and the men who were still alive had come home. The world was moving on. And John and I had walked together from the Mingos' new cottage, to see Miss Rachel's wedding.

The bridegroom stood on the steps of the church in his smart guardsman's uniform, and he put his arms around Miss Rachel. Both of them. And then he kissed her.

Next to me John cheered, like everyone else. But I had this bitter feeling rising up inside me.

Because it wasn't Julian.

And it should have been. It should have been.

I turned and ran. No one noticed me go. I ran to the other side of the church where the oak trees grow, and sat on a gravestone and put my head in my hands and let the sobs rack through me and the tears flow. Everything was wrong. And the last time I'd seen him, I hadn't even managed to be nice to him.

'Sarah!'

I knew the voice immediately. I stopped crying, and started to smile through my tears. I couldn't help it.

I felt him sit down next to me. I leant against him, feeling the stump of his arm against my back, not looking up, not daring to speak or even think. He took my hand and squeezed it.

We stayed there a long time. The birds were chattering away in the tree above, and there were shouts and cheers from the other side of the church as the bride and groom departed.

At last I turned to him. His face had changed. He had a proper moustache now, and his cheeks were thinner. And his eyes had become softer.

I moved away from him. We sat at opposite ends of the tombstone, looking at each other.

'You've grown up,' he said.

I nodded and wiped my tears with my handkerchief.

'I'm going to the grammar school,' I said. 'I got a scholarship.'

'You deserve it,' he said.

The bridal car left, and the noise of the wedding died away.

'You should have married Miss Rachel,' I said intensely. 'It should have been you.'

He laughed. It was a sweet laugh with no bitterness.

'Oh, Sarah,' he said. 'You're not still looking for happy endings, are you? Life isn't like that. You should know that, of all people. No, no. I could never have married Rachel. We'd have made each other miserable in no time.'

'But you're still friends?' I asked.

'We're friends. And we both loved Harry.'

I let the silence fall between us, as we remembered the dead. He reached out and took my hand.

'I have to say this,' he said at last. 'Sometimes someone comes into your life and they change you just by being there, by being what they are. That's what you did for me. I wanted to thank you for it.'

I said nothing. What was there to say?

'We've lost so much, Sarah, both of us. So much that will never come back. But we'll go on, won't we? The world always offers something new...'

A robin had fluttered out of the undergrowth and was sitting on a cross, eyeing us closely.

'You gave me a lot of strength, you know. You helped me live again. I can't forget that. I never will. Your friendship meant so much to me. More than I knew.'

I looked up at him in his smart wedding clothes, the tail coat and grey tie that only the upper classes wore. My own best dress felt shabby.

'We can't be friends now though, can we? Not real friends. Not any more,' I said. 'I mean, you're a gentleman. We're in different worlds...' I tailed off.

He shook his head.

'You are probably right,' he said. 'Our ways will part, I suppose. But does it matter? You are what you are to me. I'll always remember you.'

'I'll remember you, too.'

We looked at each other, and then his eyes slid away past me, and very slowly he stretched out his hand, with his finger extended. For a moment I felt all the stillness behind the birdsong and the breeze. Then the little robin hopped onto his finger and looked up at him cheekily with its black eye.

'Still the Birdman,' I whispered.

He blushed, and then he smiled, and I smiled with him.

21

What a surprise! The good things come together just like the bad.

Yesterday Sarah had her baby – a little boy. Her husband Mark telephoned from the hospital to tell me.

And today, I'd just finished washing up my breakfast, when the doorbell rang.

Judy jumped up barking, rather slow off the mark as usual. I went to open it and there was Hetty!

My Hetty! My little girl! Though she towers over me now.

'Oh, Hetty!' I said, as she put her arms round me. 'This is wonderful, but why didn't you tell me you were coming? I'd have had something ready.'

'I did tell you,' she said, looking at me strangely. 'I phoned last week. Don't you remember?'

Well, perhaps I did forget. I do forget things now. And I've had other things to think about. But I should have known Hetty would come to help with the baby anyway.

'How are they?' I asked. 'Sarah, and the baby?'

'Oh, they're doing fine. He's a gorgeous little boy. Mum, you've forgotten , haven't you? It's your birthday today! Your ninety-fifth birthday! We've all come over for your birthday!'

And suddenly there was my Trevor, a bit greyer now, and his new wife Julie, and Hetty's older girl Carol and

116

her two children, Sandra and Tom, and they were all round me, and it was almost too much for me, to be surrounded by so many loved ones, all at once.

I had to get out my hanky.

They gave me their presents and then we all went for a meal at the hotel where they're staying. Everything so smart, and lovely food, though I don't eat much. Then we sat on the terrace chatting about old times and watching the children playing with Judy. They threw a ball for her and she ran and fetched it. She's getting a bit old for those games, but she was enjoying herself.

It took me back. I was with John on the beach at Hallsands, throwing sticks for Skip...

But I couldn't have told them about it. They have their own lives.

Then they all went for a walk along the cliffs, except for Hetty.

'Get in the car, Mum,' she said. 'I'm taking you to see Sarah and the baby.'

Sarah held him up for me to see. A lovely boy. And then she made me take him in my arms. I was afraid to drop him, so I sat down with him, and looked at him, and I began to see in that tiny puckered face, the faces of all those other dear ones I'd loved and lost. And there were many. So many. Then I began to hear the voice of the sea in my ears. So I gave him back to Sarah.

'What shall I call him, Nan?' she asked.

'Whatever you like,' I said. 'There are so many nice names nowadays.'

'It's a funny thing, but I keep wanting to call him Julian. I don't know why. It just seems to suit him. And then I talked to Mark. He had a great-uncle called Julian. He was one of the early aircraft designers. Quite famous at the time, apparently.'

My head was suddenly spinning with memories.

'Was he a Birdman?' I asked.

'What?'

'A Birdman. A flying ace in the Great War. That's what we called them.'

'I don't know. He might have been.'

'It's a good name, anyway,' I said.

I think I'll have a cup of tea. It's been a very exciting day, and it's good to be back in my own little bungalow, with Judy for company, looking out over the sea.

Life keeps going on, throwing up new challenges right to the end.

I'm told there's not much left of Hallsands now. That the odd wall stands in lonely vigil, and the rock platform is eaten away by the sea. That herring gulls and kittiwakes nest where we used to play.

A few more years and it will all be gone – a story told to tourists will be all that's left.

The box is under my bed – the same one my mother

rescued from our house in Hallsands. I know now what she kept in it: my father's letters and a few mementos. She burnt them before she died, but she left me the box. It's wooden, with metal hinges and lock, rather like a treasure chest. And I too have filled it with precious things of no value – letters from my husband; old train tickets; the birth certificate of my little boy who died a baby; crayon drawings from my grandchildren; a shiny green stone.

The fireplace in my sitting room works, even though I hardly ever use it. I'll take out all those old papers and burn them in it later. I don't want anyone going through them after I've gone. Whatever they might mean to my great-grandchildren will not be what they mean to me. They are my memories, and they go with me.

When the politicians wrote on the war memorials, '**Their names live forever**', they meant well, but they were wrong. They don't, and they shouldn't either. We all have our own time, and when it's over, it's over.

It's not dark yet.

Come along, Judy, we'll go for a walk along the beach, and watch the sunset sparkle on the waves, and I'll leave a shiny green stone among the pebbles.

Then we'll walk on a bit further, up to the clifftop. I think we can manage it one last time, don't you? I'll watch the seagulls flying home, and you might sniff a rabbit.

I have a paper aeroplane, you see. It has gone yellow

*with age, but it's beautifully made, and it will still fly. I
will stand on the clifftop and hold it up and let the breeze
take it. And this time it will reach the cliff's edge and fly
on, until it disappears into the vastness of the sea.*

    The sea gives and the sea takes.

    She will take back all of us in the end.